I WOKE UP
TO A NIGHTMARE

by
Paul Fronda

I woke up to a nightmare

First published in the United Kingdom in 2016
by Paul Fronda

Western Wall Tunnel and Bedouin Information taken from Wikipedia and The Jewish Virtual Library.

Scripture quotations taken from the Holy Bible,
New International Version.
Copyright©1973,1978,1984 by International Bible Society.
Used by permission.

Cover design by Martin Smith

Edited by Sheila Fronda

Proofread by Sheila Fronda
Copyright © Paul Fronda 2016
ISBN 9780993013287

To my friend the Pastor,
Who brought the laughter out of me,
a man of great faith.
Till our next assignment,
Johnny.

FORWARD

"Greetings, Michael. It's a glorious day."

"As usual, Gabriel. I've never known Him not to make a glorious one."

"True. His mercies are new every day. I have a message for you. The word has it that we're about to make preparations for the big day."

"This is what I've been waiting for!"

"Yes, so He needs you to assign one of your best to go down and prepare the way. There's a man calling himself 'Johnny Gold' down there."

"Yes – I've heard Mordecai speak this name."

"His bravery, skills and dedication have been brought to our attention and so he has been chosen to be used as a part of the great plan. By the way, that's not his real name. There's another person, Pastor Christian Goodfellow. He is a man of great faith. So, if you haven't any questions, Michael, I'll leave it with you."

"No questions. As usual, you can assure Him it will be done."

"I will relay your assurance, Michael."

Mordecai had just finished when, from behind him, he heard someone clapping.

"Good morning, Sir. I didn't realise you were watching."

"I'm impressed, Mordecai. How many opponents this time?"

"One hundred, Sir."

"I was hoping that's what you'd say."

Mordecai was all ears.

"I have an assignment for you. This is bigger than anything you've been sent on before, Mordecai."

"I am ready, as always, Sir."

"I know you are, Mordecai. I wouldn't be asking if you weren't. You are to assist Johnny Gold and Christian Goodfellow. They have been chosen for this special mission."

"I know Johnny, Sir, but not this 'Christian Goodfellow'. May I know anything about him?"

"He's in a hospital at the moment but he will be ready to leave soon. Aquila has already gone down to prepare him and when she has done so, the two of you will assist them both."

"She's been valuable as a sparring partner before. I think we'll make a good team, Sir."

"It has been noticed, Mordecai. It's the reason we put her with you."

"When do I leave, Sir?"

"Tomorrow morning. I will have the details ready for you before you leave."

"Thank you, Sir, for this opportunity. I will not to let you down."

viii

1

Something was wrong. It was if I was on the outside of my body, looking down on an unfamiliar world: the surroundings, the people, the buildings, the driverless cars. It was as though I had been transported into a future time.

I hadn't a clue what year it was; only that it wasn't the year I last knew. But then I couldn't even remember what year that was. So what year was it? It was all so different.

Why did I have a niggling feeling of not belonging here? This was ludicrous; I had to think back. I was … I was what? There was nothing; only this unfamiliar world. There was a name that kept coming into my mind: Johnny! Who was Johnny? Did I know a Johnny? Was it *my* name?

I could hear voices. I saw two guys standing there talking. Something inside told me one was Johnny. But who was the other guy? I could only see his back. If I had a better look at him I might have a better understanding of what was happening to me. No! That's impossible, that guy, was . . . me.

As if waking from a deep sleep, I could hear a rhythmic beeping sound. The flickering of my eyes was causing a light grey to invade my world of darkness and I realised there was a shadowy figure standing over me. Then my eyes opened fully to the brightness. It was then I heard the muffled words: "So you decided to rejoin us, Christian?"

As blurred as my vision was, I could make out it was the smiling face of a young nurse. I tried to say something but I started to choke as there was something in my throat. I tried to raise my hand to my mouth but I had no strength and it fell back down to the bed.

"Leave that to me, Christian," I heard more clearly, as she slowly removed a tube from my throat.

"Welcome back, we were wondering how much longer you were going to stay away." I couldn't comprehend what she was saying. Because my throat felt like coarse sandpaper, I whispered the word: "Water . . ."

"Here. Small sips, Christian. We don't want you choking to death after all this time."

"Where am I?" I managed to whisper.

"Don't worry about that now; the doctor will be along in a minute and he will answer any questions."

I must have dozed off. As I opened my eyes I could see, standing at the bottom of the bed, a guy in a white coat reading some notes.

"Good morning, William; it's nice to meet you. I'm Doctor Jenkins. I know you will have lots of questions, but first I need to examine you and then I've a few questions for you. Is that all right?"

I gave a little grunt to save my throat, which hurt more if I spoke.

"Just follow the light, William," he said as he shone a torch into my eyes from side to side. "Good, all seems fine there. Now get some rest and I'll be back to see you in a while."

Rest. That was the last thing I needed. I felt as if I had had enough rest to last me a lifetime. I needed answers about where I was, how long I had been in this bed, and what had happened to me.

Being more focused now, I could see I was in a room of my own. There were tubes coming out of me, some of which were hooked up to the machines that surrounded me. The door opened again; it was the smiley nurse.

"Did you get your answers, Christian?"

"No, the doctor came in, read my notes, shone a light in my eyes and left. Typical doctor for you," I managed to croak.

Chuckling, she said, "I'll see if I can speed things up for you, but I can't promise. Now let's see if we can adjust the bed to a sitting-up position. I'm sure you've had long enough lying down. Now, doesn't that feel better?"

"Thanks. Hey, Smiley, why do you call me Christian and the doctor calls me William?

"When you came in, you had no ID on you, so they named you William after the medic who brought you in; I think Christian suits you more."

"Why Christian?"

"No reason," she said with a smile. "Can you remember your name?"

"No. Everything is a blur."

"Well, don't worry; I'm sure it will come back to you. Give it a little time. Meanwhile you will just have to put up with the doctor calling you William. Now, is there anything you need before I go?"

"Maybe a little more water," I replied.

I laid there for what seemed like hours waiting for the doctor to come back. I had never felt so hopeless, not being able to move or do anything about it. My agitation told me that I was probably an impatient person. If there was a lesson in patience, this was it. I was just about to resign myself that he wouldn't be back today, when the door opened and he walked in.

"Now, William, feel like a few questions? Can you remember your name?"

"No; since the nurse asked me I've been trying to remember, but I know now that it's not William."

"Do you remember anything about before the incident or how you got here?"

"What incident?"

"The police say they think you were mugged. You were found unconscious with a head wound in a dark side street. Whoever did it to you took your wallet; ring and, they assume, your phone. There was nothing on you to identify you."

"So what's wrong with me? Why is it I don't seem to have the strength to move my arms and legs?" I asked him.

"It's normal for someone who has been in a coma for . . ."

"Coma! Surely I've only been out for a little while?"

"No, William, I was about to say (before you interrupted), you've been in a coma for twelve years."

I tried to speak but the shock was too great.

"William, I know this is hard, but you are over the worst now and it can only get better for you. I'll come and see you tomorrow to talk about therapy so we can get you up and walking again. Now try and get some rest.

I laid there trying to come to terms with the fact that I had lost twelve years of my life. The next thing I knew was the voice of the smiley nurse saying, "Morning, sleepy-head. How would you like a cup of tea?"

Without thinking, I said, "I don't like tea."

"That's great, Christian. You've remembered something! Coffee it is then. The doctor said that your intravenous drip can be removed and we can start feeding you a little soup. How does that sound?"

"If that's what I need to get out of here, great. The doctor was telling me that the police think I was mugged and that would be the reason I've no ID. I got to thinking about something he said. Apparently I was wearing a ring at the time of the mugging. How would they have known that?"

Smiley stood there for a moment then made her way to the bottom of the bed to read my notes.

"It says here in the list of injuries you had that there was heavy bruising on you index finger - probably from it being forced off. Sounds like you were married. Can you remember if you were?"

As hard as I tried to remember, there was nothing. "Surely, if I was married, my wife would have been in to see me?"

"Sorry, Christian, I haven't been here long. But your visitor book says there has never been anyone come to visit you."

"I can't believe that if I *was* married, it was such a bad relationship that she wouldn't come and see me." *Maybe it was. Maybe I'm a bad person,* I thought to myself.

"There could be hundreds of reasons, Christian, but don't think the obvious."

"What's that?"

"That you're a bad person. I know you're not. Don't try to think about it too much. Your brain suffered quite an injury. The answers are still in there and it will unscramble them all eventually. One day at a time, Christian."

"Thanks, Smiley."

"Thanks for what?"

"The reassurance."

"You're welcome, Christian. I'll go and organise that soup for you."

At least I had found out two things about myself: that I didn't like tea and that I was married (or possibly divorced and still wore the ring). Or maybe I'm not divorced - but if that's the case, why hasn't she been to see me? I had so many unanswered questions. The nurse's words came back to me: "One day at a time." It was strange that she knew I was thinking that I must be a bad person. Everything was so confusing and I felt completely lost.

Even though weeks had passed and, through intensive therapy, I was up and walking and gaining strength, I still didn't have any recollection of who I was or what happened on that night that the lights went out for twelve years. The only thing that kept coming to me was a street name that I decided to write down in case it went from my mind. It might be a clue as to where I was from.

Doctor Jenkins informed me that, because of my remarkable recovery, tomorrow would be my discharge day. Was I apprehensive? Yes. But it was the day that I would be on a quest to find the answers to who I was.

"Well, Christian, it's been a pleasure looking after you.   Now, do you remember what I've told you about the changes that have taken place outside and why they want you to have a micro-implant fitted?"

"Remind me, Smiley."

"It's the law. Apart from being arrested, you will not be able to buy food or travel without it. They are expecting you downstairs at Level 2 to fit it for you. She made her way over to me and gave me a hug, and quietly whispered in my ear, "*Don't do it! God bless.*" Then she pulled away and said, "Goodbye, Christian. I hope you find your answers. Don't forget . . ."

"I know, one day at a time."

With a little chuckle and her contagious smile, she walked away.

The door opened and in walked Doctor Jenkins. "I thought I would come and say goodbye to you, William, and explain that, before we can discharge you, there is a small procedure that you must have done, which will only take five minutes. You see, things have changed since you've been here. It's a microchip that is placed under the skin in your hand."

"I know. Smiley has just explained it to me."

"Who?"

"Smiley. The pretty nurse that's been looking after me."

"What pretty nurse? Is this the same nurse that you claim to have told you how you came to be called William?

"Yes, the same one."

As far as I know, the only nurse who has been looking after you is Tony, a male nurse."

"Believe me, Doctor, I might have had a bang on the head and been out of it, but I can assure you I still know the difference between a pretty female nurse and a guy. And I tell you, I haven't had any guy in here looking after me."

There was a bewildered look on his face as he said, "So whoever it was, you've had it explained to you and you know where to go? Take these notes with you and hand them in at the desk. Because of your circumstances, the New Order has allocated a thousand credits on the chip. It will tie you over till you get settled. Now, you're sure you know where you are going?"

"Downstairs. Level Two."

"If you have any problems, you know where to come. I wish you well, William."

"Oh, Doctor Jenkins, can I've a word with you?" said the nurse at the corridor desk.

Dr Jenkins, looking at his watch, said, "It will have to be quick, Nurse. I'm behind on my rounds already."

It's about William; I think it would be better for you to see for yourself, rather than me trying to explain," she said, showing him the monitoring screen of William's room.

The monitor was showing William having a conversation with himself.

"When was this recorded?"

"Just before you went into his room, Doctor. But this has been going on since he came out of the coma."

"Why haven't I been informed of this before now?"

"I'm sorry, Doctor. I've been meaning to, but what with the amount of people coming and going, and the lack of staff, I just haven't got round to it."

"Has the male nurse left then?"

"Tony? No, Doctor. He's in one of the other rooms attending another patient."

"Do we have a female nurse called 'Smiley' working on this level?"

"Smiley? No, Doctor, definitely not. Do you think there's still something wrong with him? He's supposed to be discharged tomorrow."

"I don't think there's anything seriously wrong with him; all his vitals are fine. Although he is convinced that whoever is talking to him is real. I still think he's harmless enough to be discharged tomorrow. I don't think one more like him out there is going hurt."

I made my way downstairs to Level Two and stood outside the swing doors to the department. I stopped. Smiley's whisper, *"Don't do it!"* made me feel really uneasy about the implant, but then I thought that, if I didn't have it, I wouldn't be able to travel or eat or even survive.

Suddenly, whatever it was stopping me going through the doors, became stronger. It was then I heard the audible words, "**Leave now**." Because it sounded just like Smiley's voice, I turned around expecting to see her behind me, but there was no one there.   I quickly made my way to the ground level and the exit.

2

As I stepped out of the hospital doors, I could see things were not as I remembered. There were security cameras and uniformed police everywhere, monitoring the people going to and fro. Whether that was just outside the hospital or not, I wasn't sure. I didn't have a clue where I was going; then as I stood there I noticed people making their way to a line of taxis close by. I decided to walk over to one, hoping that if I explained my situation (and lack of money) to the driver, I could have a lift. As I opened the door, I could see that there was no driver; an automated voice said, "Destination, please."

Unsure what to do I just stood there. A voice from behind said, "You taking this one or not?" Stepping to one side, I said "No," and watched him enter the taxi and move off. The next three that came along were the same. I didn't know why, but I had a strong feeling not to get in any of them; then my attention went to one parked a distance back. I could see that it had a driver. The same voice I had heard in the hospital entered my head and said, **"This one."**

"Where to, fellow?"

11

"I'm not too sure. Do you know this street?" I said, showing him the piece of paper I had written it on.

"Yes, that's Area Five," he said.

"What is 'Area Five'?" I asked.

"Crikey, fellow. Have you been out of the country or something?"

Smiley did say things had changed. So as to not get into deep conversation, I said, "Sort of. So this 'Area Five' - is it some sort of simplified postcode?"

"I haven't heard the word 'postcode' in a while."

He looked as though he wasn't sure whether I was pretending not to know.

After a pause he said, "Yeah. The State, in its wisdom, decided to band the towns into areas, making it impossible for citizens to travel from one area into another without a chip. Supposed to be for security."

"Chip?" I repeated.

"Sir, if you are a New Order official, checking me on the State rules, you will be disappointed. I'm fluent in all New Order regulations. All my details are up to date with the system."

"No, I'm not what you call a 'New Order official'. I really don't know what a 'chip' is. Is this the 'microchip' I've been told about?"

He gave me another disbelieving look, then said, "Wow, fellow, what country have you been in? Are you saying you haven't got one?"

"Well no. Like I said, I don't really know what it is."

"Mr, if you haven't got one, you're not going anywhere. Every one who wants to travel or even buy food has to have a chip. How did you beat security getting into the country? People have been trying for years to beat the system."

I was beginning to cotton on but I needed more information. "So tell me more about the chip."

"You really don't know do you? I didn't think there was anybody left who didn't have a chip. It's an implant that is put under your skin on your hand or forehead. Each person is given a unique number - for life. The chip contains everything about you, and is stored at the Central Eye."

"Central Eye? What on earth is that?"

"It's a computer that monitors everything and everyone."

"Where is it then?"

"No one really knows. Some say it's in a nuclear bunker hidden deep underground somewhere. We don't even know what country. All we can see of it are revolving computerised 'eyes' at the top of high obelisks in all the cities. You couldn't miss them; they are all-seeing and you can't make a move without them knowing. They're even monitoring our journey right now. It's all sent back to the Central Eye. It controls everything."

"Can it hear us talk?"

"Normally it can, but with this little device here, no."

His hand went to a device on a shelf under the dashboard.

"But if you were walking past a Listening Point (dotted along the streets) it would hear anything you said and, if it was offensive to the New Order, you would be picked up and taken to a Correction, or Disposal Centre."

"Why do they need Listening Points if everyone has an implanted chip?"

"They told the people they are information terminals and they are, but what they didn't tell everyone is that they pick up what's said by the people passing by. This is a secondary precaution in case people are clever enough to interfere with the transmitters in their personal microchips.

So where have you really been, fellow? I know, from what you've said, that you haven't been in another country, because every country has the same system, now it's a One World Order."

Those words seemed familiar. "How long ago did all this happen?"

It started nearly ten years ago. So are you going to tell me then?"

There seemed to be something about this guy that gave me the confidence to confide in him. "I've been in a coma for twelve years; I woke up about six weeks ago."

"It makes sense now! I knew it was impossible to get in and out of the country without a chip, although I've been praying that I would meet someone who has. A coma for twelve years you say? Well look on the bright side: it's been twelve years that you haven't had to put up with this nightmare world, with all this monitoring."

The taxi came to a stop a little way back from a sign that said: '**You are entering Area Five'.**

"This is as far as I can take you without a chip, fellow."

"But I need to get to that address. I'm not sure, but I think it's my home."

"I've probably said too much already and I might be putting my head on the block, but something tells me you are one of the good guys. You have to be careful whom you talk to; it's hard to trust anyone.

It's been known for a brother to turn a brother into the authorities for going against the system. Even the other day it was broadcasted over the airways about a parent informing on their child who turned to Christ. Fellow, you have woken up to a nightmare. But I'm going to take a chance and help you."

"What makes you sure you can trust me? How do you know I'm not working for the so called New Order, sent out to trap people like you?"

"I must confess when you got in I wasn't sure. That's why I said all that stuff about knowing all the State regulations. But I trust in the good Lord that every decision I make is of Him, and my spirit tells me you are okay. I don't suppose you've got anywhere to stay?"

"If I could get home I would."

"Listen, you have to forget that idea for now. If you were to cross the line into that area without a chip you would be picked up and taken away. If they felt like being kind to you, you would be thrown into one of the holding pens dotted around the country till the system got around to interrogating you. Every day they show pictures of the many who are in there, as a deterrent to all who have religious beliefs or will not have the chip implanted for other reasons. Depending on how busy they are, you might be disposed of. No, I'll take you to a safe place where there are some good people left who haven't taken the chip."

"Haven't you been fitted with one?"

"No, I'm a man of many devices. My chip is false - it fools the system. It's the only way my friends and I can survive in this crazy world, and of course with God and prayer."

"You're a Christian?"

"That word alone would have you disposed of within the blink of an eye. Yes, I'm a Christian."

"I don't know why I'm going to say this, but I think I am too."

"Well, fellow, they say God takes care of his own. You could have taken any taxi, and most of them nowadays are those driverless ones, but you got into mine and it was at the back of the queue.

If you had got into one of them without a chip you would have been scanned for identity. The doors would have locked automatically and the taxi would have taken you to *them*. I've already told you what would happen next. Yes, the Lord was guiding your steps all right. I was about to go for a break, but I know the Lord had me stay a little longer in that rank for a reason and it looks like that reason was you, fellow. I think it's time I stopped calling you 'fellow' and you told me your name."

"William."

"Just William?"

"It's what the hospital named me as I didn't have any ID on me when I was brought in."

"You mean you can't remember your name?"

"Afraid not."

"Well, it will have to do. My name is Johnny Gold. Okay, William, I think it's time to go; we wouldn't want to bring attention to ourselves by staying too long outside the zone."

"By the way, *do* you know all the State regulations?"

"I make it my job to; you never know when some New World official will get into the taxi and pretend he's not tying to catch me out - like you," he finished off with a little chuckle.

"But you know I'm not."

16

"I know now, but you can't be too careful."

It was now dark and we pulled up outside a disused warehouse near a dock. I watched him cautiously get out of the taxi, making sure that nobody was watching from within the darkness. As soon as he got back in, a steel roller door in front of us started to lift and we drove in. He told me to stay in the car, then he made his way to a closed steel door. Looking around once more, he beckoned me to come over to him. He took a device out of his pocket and pointed it at the door, whereupon a green light flashed, then the door made a click and opened.

"This way," he said, as the door automatically closed behind us. We went down a fight of steel steps to be confronted with another steel door, which he opened the same way.

"We could see on the camera that you'd brought someone new with you, Johnny. Where did you find him?"

"I didn't. The Lord did," he replied to a guy sitting amongst a group of people.

"This is William; he's clean, chip free. I'll let him tell you his story later," Johnny said to them as they gathered around.

"Welcome, William. Our home is your home. I'm Brian."

I was in a large room with about twenty-five people, a mixture of women, men and some children.

"We haven't got much, but the Lord supplies all our needs, and it's a safe place. Have you eaten?

We're just about to give thanks for the food; please - sit down and eat."

I half-expected to be interrogated, being a stranger who'd come into their secret place, but no one asked any questions. They accepted me on the word of Johnny. I was just finishing my food when I heard the words, "Mark's outside the main door." Turning to the guy who said it, I saw him looking at a monitor on the wall.

"Letting you in, Mark," he said into an intercom.

It wasn't long before the door opened and in walked a tall guy with a large box. Several of the women got up from the table and took the box from him.

"It's getting harder. I think this is going to be the last of it. My contact is getting nervous about supplying so much food to me at a time. He doesn't know for sure, but he thinks he might be being watched. Don't worry, I made sure I wasn't followed. I took the long route here," he said.

"Mark, come and meet our new addition," Johnny said to him.

"Christian?" he said.

"You know me?"

"It's me – Mark. Wow, I thought I'd never see you again. What happened to you?"

I looked at him vacantly. "I'm sorry but...."

Johnny noticed my confusion. "Mark, you obviously know him. William's been in a coma; you'll have to slow down. He doesn't remember much, even who he is. You could be the break-through he needs. I suggest we all sit down."

"You're older, but I would know my pastor anywhere," he said. "And your name isn't William, it's Chris . . ."

"I'm a *pastor*?" I said, interrupting him in surprise.

"Yes. Pastor Christian, of the Church of Good Hope. You left on a mission trip to Africa; that was the last we saw of you. We knew the communication would be sketchy where you were going but, when we hadn't heard from you after two weeks, we were all concerned, especially Linda. Linda - your wife."

"So I do have a wife! Surely she wouldn't have given up trying to find me?"

"Christian, no one could be more determined than Linda; she did everything she could, trying to find you through the mission field channels, here and in Africa. But all she kept hearing was there was no record of you ever being on the flight or meeting your contact there. And I tell you, if it hadn't been for that information, she would have been out there, even though she didn't have a clue to where to look," Mark said.

"Did she not phone all the hospitals?" I said with a trace of bitterness I couldn't hide.

"She did, but on the day you disappeared there were large terrorist bombings in several towns. She feared you were caught up in it. The hospitals were overrun with casualties and dead bodies. It was mayhem. She phoned the hospitals and gave your description but the only thing they would say was that some of the victims were beyond recognition, and even then she would not accept it. She never gave up searching for you; she knew in her heart that you weren't dead."

"Where is Linda now?" There was silence, as Mark and Johnny looked at each other.

"Two years after you disappeared, in order to clamp down on 'radical religious beliefs', the Government started to tax churches so highly that

19

one by one they closed. With the help of the Lord, our church (along with a few others) managed to pay the taxes every month. When they realised that not all churches were forced to close, they accused those remaining of promoting 'extreme religious ideas' – against a law they had recently passed.

They raided our church in the middle of a service. In the mayhem that followed, some of us managed to escape to the streets and mingle with the onlookers, who were cheering the police. The last I saw of Linda and most of the others, they were being herded into vans and driven away." Mark said.

"Where would they have taken her?" I asked with a lump in my throat.

"Do you remember the holding pens I was telling you about? It would be one of those. As the church was in Area Five, it would probably have been Holding Pen Four. They allocate three areas to one pen," Johnny explained to me.

I stood up and said, "I've got to find her."

"William, I mean Christian, that was ten years ago. The reality is she's probably not there. She would have had the opportunity to deny her faith, but, by the sound of it, she would not have done that and therefore she would have been dis . . ."

Johnny didn't have to finish his words. I remembered what he told me would happen to those who didn't comply with the law.

"But I still have to try. There might just be a glimmer of hope that she's still in there. Will you help me Johnny?"

"I'll tell you what, Pastor, I'll have a look to see if there are any records of her still being there and, if she is, a few more days won't make any difference. We need time to get you fitted out with one of our chips and get you an identity. Talking about that, Mark: what's the Pastor's full name?"

"Pastor Christian Goodfellow, and a great pastor he was. The church was full every week and almost outgrowing the building."

"Excuse the pun, William, (I've got to stop calling you that), Pastor Christian, but when I said in the car that you were 'one of the good guys', I wasn't far wrong," Johnny said with a little chuckle.

"Johnny, that's the first time I've heard you laugh," Mark said.

"Is it?"

Mark called for quiet in the room and said, "Listen everyone, you know we have prayed for years for the good Lord to send us someone to lead us? Well, today He has answered our prayers and sent us a pastor, Christian Goodfellow."

I didn't have a chance to think about it. I wasn't even sure I could pastor myself, let alone twenty or so people, and anyway I was making plans to leave and find my wife. But looking around, all I could see were lost sheep that now had hope in their eyes. One by one they were coming up and hugging me.

Because there were still a lot of missing pieces that I needed answers to, I said to Mark, "Are you staying here tonight? I was wondering if you could fill me in with some details leading up to my disappearance and tell me how this world became such a crazy place."

"Sure, Pastor, if I can; what do you want to know?"

"How did all these changes take place? Who are these people in control? How did they get control? What's this 'One World Order' Johnny mentioned to me?"

"Sounds as if I had better start at the beginning, Pastor. Do you remember when the mobile phone was introduced and then the Internet - where people would send emails and surf the net, either to buy something or find information? Well, every time anyone went on it, their details were logged on a massive computer storing every bit of information about them, their hobbies, their likes and dislikes, even the food they ate. At the same time a microchip for animals was introduced, to identify them if they went astray.

Well that was the beginning of it all. We were oblivious to the real reason for all the collective data and the chip. They used the animals as a trial to see if it worked, and it did, so they developed a more powerful chip for humans but they didn't introduce it straight away. They were too devious for that, knowing that there would be opposition from a lot of people. No, they knew it would have to be done slowly if it was to work; it was all part of a master plan to create the 'One World Order."

"Out of all the things I'm trying to remember, why does that term ring a bell?" I asked Mark.

"It's probably from all the times you heard it being talked about years ago. I can hear them now - saying, "It will never happen. How wrong they were!"

"But how did the Government get the people to accept them?" I asked.

"You know, Pastor, I often tried to work out what started it all. Then I came up with a theory that it was the introduction of the credit card all those years ago. It was a new concept that made it so easy for people to acquire what they wanted immediately and many got into long-term debt due to the high interest payments. They became slaves to the corporations and, for most, dept became a way of life.

Then they brought out a card that had a chip, which made it easier and faster to use. But, every time the card was used, the information was collected to build a data base on the card holder."

"Yes, I remember. When you lay it all out like that you can see the plan, but at the time you can't."

"Precisely, Pastor. Now, in these past twelve years technology has increased beyond belief. By the way, have you noticed there are no more mobile phones?"

"You know, Mark, what with all these other changes I haven't. Don't tell me they've done away with them as well?"

"Yes. Everyone has a transmitter and receiver imbedded in the chip; it's on all the time.

"Oh, that's what Johnny was on about."

They announced that they were going to introduce a cashless society, saying that it would be more secure when buying anything and would help to keep robberies and muggings down.

The next step of the plan was to do away with the card and introduce the microchip - which is implanted under the skin; but what they didn't tell us was that the new advanced chip would monitor every move we make, giving them our location day and night. It also meant that without it you couldn't buy anything.

As they expected, there was opposition from us Christians. Of course you know, it warns in the Word that we shouldn't take the mark of the beast and that we would recognise it by the number 666. This is how clever they are: each person has a ten-

23

digit number allocated to him or herself. The 666 is placed somewhere in the number, maybe at the end or in the middle, so that it isn't obvious.

Because there was still a lot of opposition from those who did see it, they passed a law making it compulsory and, for those who didn't take it, it meant the Holding Pens.

The most devious part of the plan concerns DNA. What we didn't know was that every time someone gave blood or had a blood test, their DNA was put on a database. Then they passed a law that everyone else had to be included, and if not it was, again, the Holding Pens. Of course, any new babies are automatically added to the data.

"Holding Pens? That's a term you would associate with animals."

"You're not far wrong there, Pastor. Those in them have their human rights taken away and are considered no more than animals. They're known as 'Lowlifes'. I've heard that the conditions there are . . . well, let's just say animals are treated better.

"Didn't anyone question why these pens were being erected?"

"Those who did were told that, because the prisons were getting full, they would be temporary overflow prisons.

"So, who are these people? How did they get into power?" I said angrily.

"It was so gradual; at first people didn't realise what was going on. Most people were too busy trying to run their own lives and those who were willing to get involved with these issues were so few and weak- willed that they backed down from any conflict.

24

The people were easily led. Even though there were some Christian parties that ran for office, they too were weak and, if they'd read their Bibles, they would have seen that they were being told so. It says in 2 Corinthians 11:19:

'You gladly put up with fools since you are so wise! In fact, you even put up with anyone who enslaves you or exploits you or takes advantage of you or pushes himself forward or slaps you in the face.'

Those who wanted to run our lives got into power when the elections came around. They told people what they wanted to hear and then, once elected, they would not do it. Basically they just lied their way to power. But then the Bible says that we would be deceived. For Christians it's getting tough to survive," Mark admitted, sounding exhausted.

Without thinking, I said: "*Consider carefully what you hear'*, Mark 4:24. *The Lord says that He will not leave us or forsake us, Joshua 1:5.*

'We're hard pressed on every side, but not crushed; perplexed, but not in despair; persecuted, but not abandoned; struck down, but not destroyed.'
2 Corinthians 4: 8-9.

'So we fix our eyes not on what is seen, but on what is unseen. For what is seen is temporary, but what is unseen is eternal.' 2 Corinthians 4:18."

"That's right, Pastor. How easily we can forget those comforting words; that's what's been missing around here, a Pastor to remind us."

I couldn't believe I had quoted all those scriptures. *Where are all these words coming from?* I thought to myself.

"Pastor, things are so bad out there; they are passing laws that, even as little as five years ago,

25

would not have been acceptable. They have gone far beyond the realms of sanity. Public prayer has been made illegal, and why? Because the majority of Christians stayed quiet.

There's an 'Equality Law' they introduced that says everyone has the right to anyone's processions, which includes even your wife and family, if the other person so desires."

"No, that's just too far-fetched to believe!"

'Well, even in 1840 a French anarchist Stated that 'all property is theft' and I believe the Communists took it up as a mantra. So the idea is not new – it's just been taken a few steps further. There was a time when you could call the police if your house was broken into or someone entered it without permission. Then cuts in police funding meant that it was hard to get the police to attend when you were burgled. Now thieves have every right to enter and take what they like.

The family members of the head of the household are classed as possessions. It only applies to people that were already married before the law came out, when marriage between a man and woman became illegal. It was their way of deterring people from marrying and it is encouraged that people live together, regardless of their gender. (Yet there have even been cases of people marrying their pets!)

There was an extraordinary court case not long ago about a guy who made his way into somebody's home and made claim to his 'rights' under that law. Because the husband objected and stopped him, the guy called the State police. Because of what they saw in his house the husband didn't stand a chance. They took the husband away for 'breaking the law'.

His 'trial' was shown publicly as a deterrent to others. In fact, we recorded it. Have a look:"

"Court arises. The case is between George Grimshaw and Peter Hoperight. It is said that Peter Hoperight deliberately denied George Grimshaw his human right to come into his house and take possession of it and his family. This denial directly contravenes the Law of Equality, that all people have a right to things that don't belong to them. It is also said that he used an offensive word against George Grimshaw; I quote: 'Jesus.' This name is high on the list of 'Extremist Terms.' Such actions will not be tolerated by the New Order, whether from an individual or group. The Law of Human Rights must be upheld.

It is also noted that, when an officer of the law was called to the home of the defendant, he noticed in the house there was a Bible and various other articles of extremist content. When questioned, he claimed they belonged to his child but when the officer opened the book he could see clearly the words written: 'To Daddy on your birthday.'

Based on such evidence, the State recommends that these charges be applied:

1) Breaking the Law of Equality.
2) Using the banned term: 'Jesus'.
3) The possession of a Bible and cross.

All of the above charges have been proven against you, the second and third of which require the death sentence.   The New Order therefore commands that you be taken to a Disposal Centre and beheaded. The mother and child are to be taken to a Correction Centre and then returned to George Grimshaw."

"I cannot believe it! There's no way that charade could be called a trial. I've awoken into a nightmare world where wrong is now called right; where white has become black. Is there any good left in this crazy world?"

"Only in the groups of people like us in hiding, Pastor.

"So there are others?"

"Yes, dotted around the country, and around the world. We do communicate by our scrambled phones, thanks to Johnny. He's a genius with electronics, thank the Lord.

I've often asked the Lord why He didn't take me, along with the others, when he came and took His people to be with Him. But then, if I'm honest, even though I'd heard you preach on the subject many times, deep in my heart I didn't think it would really happen. And maybe that's the reason I didn't get taken?"

"You mean *the Rapture* happened! When?"

"About three and a half years ago. It caused so much chaos around the world. But then, there was turmoil anyway. We were on the brink of world war, earthquakes were off the scale, there were weather patterns never known before; there was also famine, and diseases that resisted known medicines.

People were looking for someone to bring peace to the world; the trouble was they chose the wrong person. He calls himself 'The Supreme One'. In the first three years he did bring peace, and people thought he was God, but it was a plan of deception. When he had the trust of people he showed his true colours. Things got worse and evil is everywhere.

Even though the Bible told us we would know the signs of the times before His coming, people were still carrying on with violence, greed, and selfishness. Then, when the Christians disappeared, people wanted answers from the Government, who came up with the explanation that aliens had taken them! If it hadn't been so serious it would be laughable, but the people bought it."

"I can't believe it! I was born again and, even though I was in a coma, I don't understand why He didn't take me. I was sure that I'd go with Him when he came," I said dejectedly.   "So, three and a half years - that makes us halfway through the tribulation."

"Yes, Pastor. When they all went, I got searching for answers in the Bible and now I know the reasons why so many, who believed they were saved, didn't make it. Most of them thought that, by going to Church on a Sunday, and saying the salvation prayer, they would be raptured, but most of them (like myself) didn't believe from their heart.

I suspect that most of the people taken were women, because if you asked a man how he came to know the Lord, he would usually answer that it was because of his wife or girlfriend. I'm sure that's why the Lord made women; He knew what us men are like, too proud to say we need help. But I know He is a God of second chances and He's coming back one day to reign on earth – so we'll be with Him then.

29

"Maybe you're right, Mark, about the women. I must confess I couldn't help noticing that there are more men here than women. But I know that I know that my wife and I believed in our hearts when we gave our lives to the Lord. Yet He didn't take me."

"Yes, Pastor; in fact I know, by the way you preached in that church, that you did. Maybe the Lord left you behind to help all the others?"

"I hope so, Mark; I hope so." I paused a while then I said, "I wonder if Linda is with Him?"

"Maybe, Pastor. So tell me, how did you get out of the hospital without having the chip?"

"A smiling angel," I said.

"An *angel*?"

"Well, looking back, it must have been. There was a pretty, smiley, young nurse who looked after me. When it was my time to leave, she explained about the chip but whispered in my ear, "Don't do it".

Then on my way to have it done, I stood outside the department, trying to figure out how I could survive without it, when I heard an audible voice saying, "Leave *now*!" Then I found myself outside the hospital doors.

"But, what makes me think she was an angel?"

"Something the doctor said. When he mentioned the chip, I told him the pretty nurse had already told me about it and he assured me that the only nurse who'd attended me was a male nurse!

She also said that 'Christian' suited me more that 'William'. She smiled as she said it, so she *knew* my real name! Why didn't she just tell me?"

"It makes sense to me, Pastor. By not telling you, she has protected you from telling the hospital your real name. If you had known it and had the chip implanted, you'd be known to the system. The Lord had a plan for you, Pastor, and still has. And, if I'm quoting the scripture right, it says in Psalm 91:1 that He will send His angels to watch over us."

"There's something that puzzles me, Mark. Both you and Johnny told me that if I didn't have a chip, it would have been picked up by the State's cameras, yes?"

"That's right."

"Well, how come, when I walked out of the hospital without one, nothing happened?"

"That's a mystery to me, Pastor. Johnny! The Pastor is asking a good question here. How come he didn't get picked up by Security when he left the hospital without a chip?"

"That's simple - a miracle. It was the only way. Unless of course he had one of my 'God chips', which he obviously didn't. No, it definitely was a miracle."

"There's your answer, Pastor, and I'm in agreement with Johnny."

As I sat there listening to Mark, I felt a little tug on my sleeve from behind. I turned, to see a young girl standing there.

"Pastor," she said, "Can I pray for you?"

"Why, sure."

"Lord Jesus, please give our Pastor wisdom and strength to lead us and please make him better. Amen."

The little girl's short prayer brought a lump to my throat. "Thank you . . .?"

"It's Gabby, Pastor," she told me.

"Thank you, Gabby. It's been a long time since I've heard such a beautiful prayer. I bent down and

31

gave her a hug. Well, Mark, I think I'll turn in, if you can show me where."

"Sure thing, Pastor."

3

I awoke to my first morning in this new place. It was comfortable but it lacked the facilities of the hospital, although the smell of bacon cooking more than compensated for any lack.

"Good morning, Pastor. I hope you had a comfortable night? We thought that, now we have a Pastor, we'd use up the last of the bacon to celebrate," Mark announced.

Before I had a chance to thank him, the words: "Come, let's give thanks to the Lord for this new day and for the food," came out of my mouth. It was so spontaneous that I knew such words must have been natural for me to say. My life was slowly being pieced back together.

Even though there seemed to be a very small amount of bacon, there was enough for everybody. Something told me that this had happened before but on a grander scale. I couldn't help smiling. "Well, Mark, what's the schedule for the day?" I asked.

"Some of us have jobs and will be leaving to go to work, others will go and get provisions and the women stay to home-school the children. It's too dangerous for the children to go out, in case they say something that would give our position away."

"I would have thought that He would have taken all the children, especially the young ones."

"He did, Pastor; it was so traumatic for the parents and still is."

"So why didn't he take these two children?"

"Little Gabby and her sister, Jenny, were born after the event. The State has no knowledge of them; they were born here.

Changing the subject, I asked, "Do we have an escape exit from here, if we should need it?"

"Come with me, Pastor. Now you are one of us, you need to know."

Mark led me to the back of the building. "Watch, Pastor, your life could depend on it." He put his hand on a pressure switch on the wall and the wall slid to one side, revealing a fight of stairs leading down to the river, which came into the warehouse basement. At the bottom of the stairs were moored two high-speed motor launches.

"That's our escape, if we ever need it. The beauty is, because of the steel roller-door to the outside, it can't be seen from the river. Pretty good hey, Pastor?"

"And you need someone to lead you? You seem to be doing a good job already," I said.

"It's the spiritual aspect, Pastor; we need encouragement, to give us hope and a vision."

I agreed; even in the good times we all need that. *'For without hope and a vision, the people perish. Proverbs 29:18'* came to me.

We made our way upstairs; a few of the others had already left, including Johnny.

"How long before Johnny comes back?" I asked Mark. "I was hoping he would take me to find my wife."

"Pastor, I hope you don't mind me saying, but we don't know for sure if the Lord took her - in which case there's no point in looking for her; best wait till Johnny gets back. He did say that he would do some searching. I would think that, as usual, he's gone off somewhere. If he *has* found her, it will be to collect resources for the journey. Without them, Pastor, I don't think you'll make it. Trust me, he knows what he's doing."

The hours went by. Without much to do the day went very slowly. My boredom was ended abruptly as one of the women announced: "Johnny's outside!"

I stood anxiously at the steel door, waiting for it to open. Johnny came in carrying a suitcase.

"Sorry I've been so long. I had to wait till it was dark, but it was worth it. I think I've got all we need to get us in the pens."

"So you found her then?"

"Yes - late last night. You had turned in, so I couldn't tell you. But yes, she's being held in Pen Four."

"Well, Pastor, that answers your question. I guess that, like yourself, He left her here for a reason."

"As much as I long for her to be with me, part of me wishes that He had taken her from this crazy place, Mark."

"So what did you get, Johnny?" Mark asked him.

"God opened all the doors for me, with the timing and the connections," Johnny said, opening the case.

35

"Try this on for size, Pastor," he said, handing me what looked like a police uniform.

"Why do I need this?"

"If we're to get into one of those pens, trust me, you'll need it. Here's your ID badge: Mr Lucas Jennings, Security Division, Level One clearance from HQ Central. And I'm your driver."

"What? Are we going to turn up in a taxi?"

"Give me some credit, Pastor. Trust me, I have something special for that. I've got some hacking to do, into the State mainframe, and I reckon we'll be ready to go in the morning."

I didn't have a clue what he was doing on the computer so I gave up watching him and helped with getting the evening meal ready.

"You joining us, Johnny?" one of the women said to him.

"Nearly there, just a final click of the button. There - all done. The ID badges will get us through and the papers are in order."

"So tell me, Johnny, where did you learn to do all this?"

"I used to be a computer programmer, working for one of the big IT companies owned by the Government. I was working on a new program that was way different to what I was used to. What made me suspicious was that normally it would be just me working on a program from start to finish, but this time I was only given a section to work on. Yet, even from the bit I had been given, I could see that this was scary stuff. It was bordering on the mind control of every individual in the country. I knew it wasn't right.

So one night I told them that I needed more time on my section and asked if I could work on and finish

36

it. They had no objections; in fact I was encouraged to do so. Having put a few safety measures in place on my computer (so they couldn't detect what I was about to do), I hacked into my colleagues' computers to see what their sections would reveal.

It was much scarier than I first suspected. It was a program that was intended to install fear into everyone's subconscious   that they couldn't exist without the Government. This would be reinforced every time they went online.   It was even going to be applied to online games for children.

I knew I had to get out, for I didn't want any part of it. As no two programmers knew what the other was writing, and due to the way it was encoded, they considered it to be safe, so they had no concerns about me giving my notice to quit.

Because I didn't want my details left on the system, I erased my data and rewrote my new identity as 'Johnny Gold', undercover security agent for the New Order. My job was to integrate with the people, under the guise of a taxi driver, but I had to make sure that I had covered every trace of my activities before I assumed my new identity."

"Why a taxi driver, Johnny?" I had to ask.

"Well I knew that the Security Department had stepped up surveillance on 'religious extremists' so I wrote my details on the system as a taxi driver. You see, people without a chip can't use the automated taxis so, by having one with a driver here and there, the State think they'll trap people who think they'll be safe. My job would be to get them to confide in me and then turn them in to the State but, as you know, it put me in a position to be there for people who need help."

"I was thinking about that - it didn't make sense to me that they would leave one with a driver. So what's your real name?" I asked.

"Nobody knows that, Pastor, only me. It's safer that way, and anyway I quite like the name 'Johnny Gold'; it's got a ring to it, don't you think?"

I couldn't help having a little chuckle. "If you think so, Johnny. What time are we leaving in the morning then?"

"Just after nine, when all the chaos on the roads has died down. You need to get some sleep, Pastor; we have a busy day tomorrow and you'll need a clear mind.

4

I was woken from a deep sleep by Mark.

"Time to get up, Pastor; breakfast is on the table. We have some work to do; don't forget to put the uniform on."

I walked into the main room to see them all looking at me in my uniform.

"If I didn't know better, Pastor, I would be convinced that you were one of the New Order officials," Mark said smiling.

"I wouldn't know one if I saw one, Mark."

"Trust me, Pastor, you'll know when you see one. They're hybrids - a mean looking lot, not a bit of compassion in them. I know there's not an ounce of meanness in you, but for you to pull this off, you'll have to find some and show it on your face."

"What do you mean hybrids?"

"Do you remember when they messed around with cloning sheep and other animals? Well they secretly engineered a hybrid human by altering their DNA. A person without feelings that wouldn't feel pain, highly intelligent and strong, and they obeyed without question but they all had one thing in

39

common. Each one has this expressionless, mean look on its face – if that makes sense. I think it must be something to do with the engineering."

Looking around, I said, "Where's Johnny now?"

"He's gone to get the transport. You'd better get your breakfast down you, Pastor; he'll be back soon," one of the other men said.

It wasn't long before the door opened and a uniformed Johnny came in.

"All fit, Pastor? Let's get going."

As I was just about to go through the door, Johnny said, "One minute, Pastor; give me your hand, this might sting for a second."

Before I realised what was going on, he said, "There - now you're legal."

"What did you do?" I said, rubbing my hand.

"I fitted you with a chip, identifying who you are."

"What! Take it out! I'll not have the chip in me."

"Calm down, Pastor. It's one of mine (that I designed); it's what I call a 'God chip'. It fools them and enables us to get around outside."

"Amazing," I said with a sigh of relief.

"Pastor, before you go, can we pray for you?" Mark said. "Father, we pray for Pastor Christian and Johnny, that you would protect them in what they are about to do; that you would blind the eyes of the enemy so as their true identity would not be revealed. Also that Pastor Christian's wife, Linda, would be at the place and they will be able to rescue her and bring her back here safely. Amen. God be with you both."

"Thank you, Mark," I said, giving him a hug.

We made our way outside and there waiting was a black official-looking car.

"Not bad hey, Pastor? I said I had a little something special to travel in. What better than the genuine thing, a New Order car?"

"How did you manage that?'

"I have my means."

As Johnny opened the rear door for me, he gave me a briefcase.

"You might want to study the contents, so that you're briefed up on who you are and what we're doing at the pen. There's no room for errors. Don't forget: when you speak, speak with authority and have that mean, vacant look on your face. If you do, we might just pull this off."

As Johnny drove, I memorised the contents of the papers.

"This 'Lucas Jennings' I'm supposed to be - is he real?" I asked.

"Oh yes, he's real. As we speak, he's on a plane." Looking at his wristwatch, he said, "And about now he'll be landing in Germany."

"What's he doing there?"

"I sent him an official email yesterday, requesting his presence at a meeting at HQ Germany. That means we'll have about two hours before all . . . (excuse the term, Pastor), all hell breaks loose."

"What do mean?" I said, my voice betraying my concern.

"When he gets there and finds out that it wasn't an HQ request, they will think it's an internal mistake and it will be investigated; but the minute you use your chip, as I said, all hell will break loose."

"Why would I use my chip?"

"Do you remember what I told you? Everything involves using the chip in this age, especially where we're going. We'll have about the time it takes for an email asking for confirmation of the usage of the chip. I would guess, Pastor, about ten minutes to get out of there."

"No pressure then. Is this the car that's officially allocated to him?"

"Yep," he said with a smug smile.

"How did . . ."

"Don't ask, Pastor; let's just say that I'm a stickler for detail in all that I do. That way, if ever we should be stopped, all the paperwork ties together. No loose ends, Pastor."

"I understand all that, but I'm intrigued to know how you managed to get hold of his car?"

"It's not hard for an IT expert like me. No seriously, the weakness of the One World System is that it's so big. It's a case of the left hand not knowing what the right hand is doing in all its departments across the world. Providing you know how, it's not hard to hack into. All I did was send a notification to the Transport Department of HQ that the car had a fault and would be collected for investigation by the Service Department (yours truly: me). That's where I was early this morning."

"So it's as easy as that - if you want something you just do it?"

"Not easy, Pastor. I have to work at it," he said, smiling. "But, if I was the vindictive type, I could cause a lot of chaos to the System."

"But surely that would be a good thing, wouldn't it?"

"No. Where there is chaos, there's anarchy; better the devil you know that the one you don't. At least we know what the danger out there is for us. As bad as it is, without some sort of government, it would be worse for us. This way I have some control."

"It's a good job then that you're with us, Johnny."

"I thank the Lord, Pastor, that He's given me the wisdom."

A computerised voice announced that our destination was approaching. We came over the brow of the hill and on our left there was a high fence of barbed wire. As the car approached the guarded gates, Johnny said, "You might want to pull the brim of your cap down over your face."

Instantly I looked at the face on my identity badge. *Why didn't I check it before we set off?* I only had time to say, "Johnny, this photo!"

"Don't worry about it; the guard might not even notice," was his reply.

Don't worry! I could have killed him if I wasn't a pastor. *Any minute now I could end up with all the others inside that pen*, I thought to myself.

The words **"Trust in me"** entered my head. It was as if someone was sitting alongside me and whispering into my ear. Convinced it was Smiley, I said, "Is that you?" There was no answer, which made me think I'd just imagined it because I was desperate.

We stopped at the gate. I pulled the cap down over my face as low as I could without making it look too suspicious. I lowered myself down into the seat and pretended to read the paper, keeping my head down. The guard spoke to Johnny through the window. "Papers!" he demanded. Johnny handed them to him; then I heard the guard say, "Sorry, Sir, I should have recognised the car. Open the gate!" he shouted to the man in the booth.

As we went through the gates I could see out of the corner of my eye that he was saluting us.

"What did he mean: 'I should have recognised the car'? Are you telling me they know Lucas Jennings here?"

"I doubt it. No, it was the official headed paper and the HQC on the number plate. I should think anyone visiting from HQ causes them to panic, but I think it's probably rare they have a visit."

At the second gate were two guards waving us through.

"That's service for you, hey Pastor?"

We stopped outside the building and Johnny played the part of my driver, opening the door for me.

"Mean look, Pastor!" he whispered to me as I got out and made my way to the building while he stayed with the car. By my reception from the men at the doors, I knew that the guard had radioed through to say that HQ was on the way. They escorted me to the office where the officer in charge stood up and saluted me from behind his desk.

"Sir!" he said, "We don't often have the pleasure of a visit from HQ. How can I be of service?"

"You don't know why I'm here? Don't you read your emails?" I said with all the arrogance and authority I could muster up.

"No, Sir. I mean yes, Sir. Of course, Sir, the email," he said, looking at his computer in a fluster. "Er . . . there doesn't seem to be anything from HQ, Sir."

"What sort of an incompetent set-up are you running here, (I looked at his badge to see his name) Officer Drake?" I snarled at him.

"It might have gone to my assistant; I will track it down, Sir. Oswald, get in here now!" he shouted to his assistant next door.

A nervous, thin-faced man came hurrying in, "Yes, Sir?"

"You're forgetting yourself, Oswald! There's a senior officer in the room from HQ. Salute, man!"

"Sorry, Sir," he said to me, standing to attention.

"How is it that I wasn't informed of a senior officer visiting today? There's an email from HQ; find it and bring it here, Oswald!" his senior shouted at him.

"Yes, Sir!" Oswald saluted and hurried away.

I summoned up an angry voice: "If you think I've got all day to listen to your futile excuses, man, I'll have you removed from your post before you know what's happened. I'm here to pick up a prisoner, a 'Linda Goodfellow', brought in nine years ago."

"Nine years? Nobody is kept here that long, Sir."

"Our information says otherwise, Officer Drake."

"But, Sir . . ."

"Are you saying that HQ is as incompetent as your office and we haven't got our information right, Drake? If this prisoner isn't brought here in five minutes, I'll have *you* put in one of those cells! What's it going to be, Drake?"

"Sir, as you know of course, all prisoners are recognised by a number; they don't have names," he said, nervously. "If you could let me have the number, the system will show me where she is," he said, paused at the computer.

I had to think fast; I didn't have a number. "Surely, man, numbers weren't allocated nine years ago; it was just names?" I was playing a long shot and under my breath I was praying I was right.

"Well I think so, Sir."

Keeping up the authority in my voice, I said, "Think so? What sort of answer is that, man? Either you know or you don't!" I knew I had him; if he said again that he didn't know, it would reveal his incompetence and he daren't do that for fear of his job, or of me carrying out my threat.

"Yes, Sir, you're right. I will look further back on the system. With a look of amazement, he said, "Yes, Sir, the system reveals that she is in one of the inner cells; I don't understand how that is possible - she should have been disposed of years ago." Obviously worried that he was displaying more ineptitude, he said enthusiastically, "I'll have her brought up right away, Sir."

He picked up the phone and made a call.

I paced up and down looking at my watch, to let him see that I wasn't a person to be kept waiting. I had about fifteen minutes to get out of there before (according to Johnny) the real Lucas Jennings would be told that he wasn't summoned to a meeting, and the game would be up for me and Johnny. "How much longer, Drake? I'm not used to being kept waiting."

"I am sorry, Sir; I'm sure they will be here in a minute with the prisoner."

No sooner had he said that, the door opened and what appeared to be Linda walked in with a guard on each side of her. The flashbacks I'd had of Linda were of a beautiful, long-haired woman, but what stood before me was a handcuffed, gaunt figure with her head shaved and dressed in a filthy orange overall, with a large black C printed on it.

I'd been concerned that, even after all these years, there might be a chance that she could

46

recognise me and call out my name. As slim as it was, I couldn't take the risk. As much as it hurt me to say it, I commanded that her eyes be kept towards the ground.

"Sir, I shouldn't think she could see anything. All prisoners in those inner-cells are kept in darkness; she hasn't seen the light of day in all these years."

I had to hold back the tears. "Take her to my car," I said to the guards, whereupon they both looked to their superior for confirmation. "Now!" I bellowed.

Drake nodded his head and they quickly took her out of the room. I was just about to follow when Drake said, "Sir, I will need your mark here for release of a prisoner."

Mark? What does he mean mark? Under pressure to get out of there, I couldn't think. I had to try the authority approach again, praying it would work.

"I haven't got time for that, Drake; I'm on a deadline to get her back to HQ."

"Sorry, Sir, but it's protocol. I cannot allow the release of a prisoner without your hand mark.

Then I remembered what he meant. Of course, nothing could be done without the chip. But if I put my hand over the scanner attached to his computer, he would see immediately that my face wasn't that of the real Lucas Jennings. And even if, by a huge miracle, he didn't, I would have only minutes before the 'central eye' computer was notified that someone else was using Lucas Jennings' identity and an alarm would be flashing across Drake's computer screen.

The thought went through my head: *could I make a run for it? Would Linda be in the car by now?* Even if she was and we made it through the first gate, by that time they would have notified the guards at the main gate. A voice entered my head. ***Pray.***

"*Lord a little help here, please!*"   My thoughts were interrupted by*:* "Sir, your mark please."

I walked back over to the scanner and held out the hand that contained Johnny's chip. The same voice that had entered my head before, said: **"Trust in me."** I felt huge relief that this was going to be okay.   The scanner beam went over my hand. Drake looked at my face, not saying anything for what seemed like ages; then said, "Thank you, Sir. Have a good trip."

Without answering I made my way out to the car as fast as I could. Looking at my watch, we had minutes to make it through both gates.   I was fervently hoping that they would repeat the same level of protocol as before.

Once in the back of the car, I'd hardly closed the door when Johnny drove off towards the gate. Just as I'd hoped, they were open and we were acknowledged by salutes. The main gate also was wide open with a parade of salutes from the guards.

Able to relax a little, I turned to Linda at my side, who still had her head bowed. "Linda, don't be scared; it's me – Christian. You're safe now."

She didn't say a word. I held her hand and repeated gently, "Linda, it's me - your husband, Christian."

"Christian?" came a barely audible reply.

"Yes, Linda; it's really me."

5

I could see that we were approaching the outskirts of the town when we pulled off the road into a quiet lane bordered by trees. "Why are we stopping, Johnny?"

"Changing cars, Pastor; they will be looking for this one, and the minute we enter the town the cameras will pick us up. Here, put these sunglasses on Linda; they will help with the brightness."

We got out of the car, and there tucked away in the trees was his taxi. "How did you manage that? Don't say it. Details," I said, amused, before he had a chance to answer.

"I think you're getting to know me, Pastor." He unlocked the boot and took out a change of clothes for us. "I didn't know what size Linda was so I brought her a large hooded coat to cover up the prison overalls; see if you can get her to put it on. Before you do, we'd better do something about those handcuffs."

We were on our way back to the safe house, and Linda hadn't said a word in spite of me holding her hand, and trying to reassure her that things were going to be all right now. I could see that it was going to take a little more than that; after all, nine long years of being locked away in a dark cell isn't something that you get over in five minutes. After my own experience of adapting to life after the darkness of a coma, I knew it would be hard for her. I had to be patient, just as I had had to be with myself. It would take time to adjust but, for me, the reassuring thing was that I would be there for her.

The outer steel door rose and we drove in. Putting my arm around her, I guided her down the stairs to the inner room. As the door opened there was a mighty cheer from the others.

"Praise God, Pastor! Praise God! He brought you back safely," one of the women said, as she rushed over and hugged us.

"This is Linda, everyone. My wife."

"Hello, Linda. I'm Annie; let's see if we can get you into something a little more comfortable," she said, taking her hand.

I could see Linda pulling her hand away, which to me was natural considering the ordeal she had been through.

"It's okay, Linda. Annie will take care of you," I said. My voice seemed to reassure her and she let Annie take her into the other room.

"Something to eat, Pastor?" asked Mark.

"I'll wait and eat with Linda, if that's all right, thank you."

"Well, I won't say no!" Johnny said, sitting down at the table.

50

"Before you do, I have some questions for you," I said sitting, down with him. "I thought you were a stickler for detail?"

"I am," he said smiling, as if he knew what I was about to ask.

"How come the face on the screen wasn't mine when my chip was scanned? Did you know that it wouldn't be mine?"

"I had to keep *his* face on it, otherwise it would have given the game away. If someone had known him, they would have known that someone was tampering with the system. It's all in the detail."

"Well, if they *had* known him, the game would have been over straight away! But what I don't understand is, Drake looked straight at my face after looking on the screen. How could he not see that it wasn't the same face?"

"Don't you remember our prayer before you left, Pastor? We asked that the eyes of the enemy would be blinded to your true identities. It's obvious - God answered our prayers," Mark said.

"As I said, Pastor, don't worry, trust me," Johnny said.

"It's obvious - trusting you had nothing to do with it. It was God answering prayer."

"Well, yeah, but I helped a little, didn't I?"

I knew he was expecting an answer but I went on to say, "I can see now that God (with a tiny bit of help from Johnny) was in it all the way; even Drake said he didn't understand how Linda was still there after all that time. And the icing on the cake was: God even had the enemy saluting us. I should think that made someone down there angry," I said smiling.

"Amen, Pastor. Amen," said Mark.

While sitting there waiting for Linda to appear, I couldn't stop thinking about something that Johnny had just said; it was the words: 'Trust me', which took me back to the pen gate. I had been convinced that it was Smiley's voice, and then thought it could have been just my imagination; but maybe it was Johnny. Yet I had heard the same words in the office just before I was about to have my chip scanned, and Johnny wasn't in the room.

Then words came into my mind that seemed to explain: '**You are living in a time, Christian, when the supernatural has invaded the natural, making all things possible**.'

The door opening interrupted my thoughts and Linda came in with Annie.

"What do you think, Pastor? Doesn't she look trendy?" Annie said.

Linda was standing there in a tracksuit, baseball cap and dark glasses. "Like a pop star," I said, "but then she was always a star to me."

I could see a little smile break forth on her face. I got up and took her by the hand and sat her down beside me. "We have so much to talk about, but first things first, let's pray and then eat."

"Come everyone, let's give the pastor and his wife a little space so they can be together; they have a lot to catch up with," Mark announced.

I was up early and left Linda sleeping; I could see that some of the others had already gone to their places of work. Mark, as usual, was busying himself with organising the work rota.

"Do you know anything about Johnny?" I asked Mark.

"Only that he found each of us out there. Like you, Pastor, each of us was picked up in his taxi and brought here. You never know whom he's going to bring back with him. We know Johnny isn't his real name but it doesn't matter to us; all we know is that you feel an overwhelming assurance that you can trust him with your life. Actually, something's changed about him since you've been here. He's developed a great sense of humour, don't you think?"

"Yes. Well, obviously I don't know what he was like before. So, we don't have any background on him at all?"

"No, Pastor; he gives very little away. As I said, we have no need to ask questions about him; we just know we can trust him. It's strange though - he always seems to be one step ahead of the State police. It's as if he knows what they're going to do before *they* do; and the way he hacks into their computers, well ... I thank God for the man. Why do you ask, Pastor?"

"Oh, it's okay; it's just something he said."

"Pastor, I think someone wants to see you," Mark said smiling. I turned around and Linda was standing there. "Morning Sleepy-Head, did you sleep well?"

"What time is it?"

"Past 10 o'clock. I didn't want to wake you; you looked as if you needed it. So how did you sleep?"

"I thought I was having the same dream that I had every night – that I was free. But when I woke I could see that I was in a different place. Christian, tell me I'm not dreaming; that this is real."

"Putting my arms around her, I said, "It's real Linda."

"Tell me about this place."

53

"It's a safe house, safe from the evil that's outside. Apparently there are many of these places scattered around the world. It's reassuring that we're not on our own; there's still hope. I know that when Jesus returns, He will sort this world out."

"I can't wait, Christian! But what about meanwhile?"

"We pray and take one day at a time. God has given us people here to pastor, Linda."

"How long before we can go outside? It's been so long. All the time I was locked away, I relived the times we would go for walks in the park and away on weekend breaks. Has it changed terribly out there?"

"I'm afraid it has, Linda. It's too soon for us to venture out; getting you out of that place has upset the system. They will be looking for us; and, until Johnny fixes us up with new identities, we'll have to stay put. But, as soon as he does, I promise you I'll take you for that walk. Anyway, you're not strong enough yet; we need to build you up, and on that subject - breakfast?"

"Pastor, have you thought about what's next for you and your wife?" enquired Mark.

"That would be up to the Lord, Mark, but one thing I do know: it's not hiding behind closed doors. I didn't get left behind for nothing; it has to have been for a purpose."

The weeks had passed, and although Linda was still not back to full strength mentally and physically, she was making progress; as was I - encouraging the small flock that the Lord had provided me with, and that I was grateful for. Yet I had been used to pastoring several hundred, and felt that I needed to do more with my time. But I was in the Lord's hands; I knew that, when the time was right, He would give me the opportunity to do something specific for Him. Meanwhile, I knew that if I would be faithful with small things, He would give me bigger things.

Johnny was sitting at the taxi rank, wearing headphones and lost in the sound of his favourite worship song, when from the rear seat came a familiar voice: "You're always listening to the same old song, Johnny."

Johnny looked in the rear view mirror. "Hello Mordecai. Don't tell me - another assignment for me?"

"Yep."

"So how are things up there?"

"Intensifying, Johnny; not long now."

"I knew, by the way things were going here, it wouldn't be long. So what's this assignment you have for me?"

"Not just for you; it's for you and Pastor Christian. You are both to go to Jerusalem and, before you say anything, this is an important one. It's your biggest assignment yet."

"But you know I like working on my own. And Jerusalem!"

"I know you do; but, as dedicated and brave as you are, it's said that you are lacking laughter in your life. He made you with a great sense of humour, and having the Pastor with you, will help bring it back."

"How can a Pastor, of all people, do that?"

"Well think back, since you've know him - haven't you laughed?"

"You know, I must admit, I've had a chuckle or two. Okay - but *Jerusalem*, Mordecai?"

"I know. Jerusalem's a big ask, but He wouldn't have assigned you if He didn't think you could do it. Anyway, it will be Him doing it *through* you both. All He's asking is for a willing heart. Where's that strong faith you've had in the past, Johnny? Have I not been with you on every assignment?"

"Sure. I'll do it, but I'm a bit surprised He wants the Pastor to go; he's only just found his wife, and having been apart for so long, what makes you sure he will want to go?"

"He will; he's a great man of faith. It's his faith and your knowledge of Jerusalem, and of course your bravery, that are necessary to pull it off. This Pastor is a man who knows only one purpose: that is to serve in any way he can, regardless of the cost. The assignment details are in this envelope."

"You obviously know there's a small problem with the Pastor leaving the safe house without being picked up on the system?"

"I don't have problems."

"Yes I know that, but it's his face. I can give him an ID, but it's tying up the face with the numbers. I won't use the word 'problem' then, let's say small *issue*."

"Didn't he get away with it at the compound?"

"Yes."

"Well?"

"Are you saying you are going to make that work every time?"

"Not me - Aquila."

"If you don't mind me asking, who's Aquila?"

"The Pastor's angel. Now, are you finished with trying to find problems? I have something for you.

Take care of these. They come directly from the Throne Room of God."

Johnny twisted round and held out his hand. He watched as two tiny blue sapphire discs started to materialise in his hand. "Can I ask what they are?"

"They are microdots that contain His Holy Word. What you are to do with them will be revealed in the assignment details when needed."

"When do we go?"

As there was no reply, Johnny knew that Mordecai had gone. *Typical of you, Mordecai, never finishing a conversation*.

"It's all in the envelope!" came a voice out of the air.

Johnny called back, "By the way, I *like* that song."

A distant voice replied, "Good. I put it there."

Johnny opened the envelope and read its contents. Quickly he made his way back to the safe house.

"You're back early, Johnny," Mark said.

With urgency in his voice, Johnny said, "Where's the Pastor, Mark?"

"He's in his room praying."

"Good, were going to need all the prayer we can get."

"That sounds ominous," Mark said.

Johnny didn't reply but sat down at his desk and re- opened the envelope. Mark knew by Johnny's demeanour not to disturb him.

"Is that Johnny's voice I heard?" I said coming into the room.

"Over here, Pastor. I need to talk to you."

"You sound serious, Johnny."

"What would you say if I said I've been assigned a job that involves you?"

"I would say 'great!' I was only saying earlier that I need to do something, rather than being here in hiding. What is it?"

"Rather than try to explain it, I think it's better if you sit down and read this. Then let's see if your answer is 'great'."

Having read it, I said, "Who gave you this?"

"Mordecai."

"I've got to ask, Johnny; who is Mordecai?"

"Mordecai is a messenger from above."

"I love your humorous nature, Johnny, but can we be serious just for a bit?"

"I am being serious, Pastor. Whenever Him up there wants me to do something, He sends Mordecai along to tell me, and somehow I get a feeling he's there getting me out of trouble when it comes. He always appears in the back of my car - as he did this morning."

"What does he look like?"

That's the thing, Pastor; I've never seen him, I just hear his voice. The first time I heard him I jumped out of my skin; I turned around but there was no one there. I thought I was going over the edge or something. But he explained that, when the time is right, he will reveal himself to me. There was one time when he was talking to me that I thought I would take a sneaky look in the rear view mirror; but all I could see was a bright light."

"So how long has this Mordecai been visiting you?"

"Since just after everyone disappeared. He told me what he wanted me to do, like finding this place and bringing the lost strays here. It was then I was given the ability to be one step ahead of the authorities. So, what do you think, Pastor? Mordecai seems to think you would be up for the assignment."

"Before I answer that, does Mordecai go with you on every assignment?"

"Yes, he's always there"

"Was he there when we broke Linda out?'

"Yes, why do you ask?"

"It's just that when we stopped at the gate, it felt like someone whispered in my ear the words: "Trust in me.""

"That sounds like the sort of thing Mordecai would do, Pastor, although I don't know why, as he is assigned to me. It was most probably your angel."

"*My* angel?"

"You surprise me, Pastor, asking that. We've all got an angel assigned to us."

Smiley came into my thoughts.

"So, the assignment, Pastor. Is it a 'yes'?"

"I'm not sure how dangerous it will be, but if it's from *Him* then I know we'll succeed, especially after getting Linda out of that place. And anyway, I always wanted to go to Jerusalem."

"Me too," Pastor. I've always wanted to go again, but I was hoping it would be under different circumstances. So let's go over the details."

"You have been before?"

"Yes; it was many years ago, in better times."

"The instructions say that we're to make our way to an underground chamber way down beneath the new temple, where the source of power is that controls The Eye. Do you remember I said that no one knows where the main Eye is located, only that it's buried somewhere deep down? So now we know. It makes sense for it to be there, as the Antichrist is based there in the temple."

"So the new temple did get built then, as the Bible said it would?"

"Yes, Pastor, and the Antichrist revealed himself as the Man of Peace. He fooled everyone. As I read it, Pastor, we're to insert the sapphire discs into the mainframe of the Eye and get out of there."

"What is the purpose of the discs?"

"It says they prophecy the Word of God; everyone in the world will hear it non-stop for 1,260 days."

"Where are the discs?"

As Johnny took them out of a small pouch they radiated with a glowing power from the centre until they lit up the room.

"Mordecai said that they came from the Throne Room."

"Can I hold them, Johnny?"

"Sure, Pastor, after all He trusted us both with them."

"So, how do we pull this off, Johnny?" I said, mesmerised by the aura surrounding the discs.

"We don't. He does, Pastor, but what we do, is to create some new identities for ourselves, to get us there. That is the easy bit; for the rest we're on a wing and a prayer."

"Did you notice, Johnny, what the title at the top of the assignment paper is?"

"No, I went straight to the instructions."

"Have another look."

"The Two Witnesses. That's from Revelations, as you know, Pastor."

"Yes, Chapter 11 to be precise."

"I hope we're not them; they get killed in the end," he said, chuckling.

"No, I can assure you, Johnny, we're not them. Anyway, they come back to life and are taken to Heaven."

"But, seriously, Pastor in the natural realm this is a one-way trip; it might be prudent to explain to Linda that you can't be sure that you will be coming back."

"But we're not in the natural realm; we'll be working in the supernatural. Why do you talk like that, Johnny? One minute your full of faith, then you're talking doubt."

"Sorry, Pastor. I do have faith; it's just something Mordecai said about the assignment. He said that you were a man of great faith and that you would do it regardless of the cost. Those last four words tell me there is a chance that we won't be back."

"Well, if we don't, we'll be going home one way or the other. As much as it would sadden me to leave Linda, especially when I've just found her, to be with the Lord . . ."

"Tough call, Pastor. I've no one to leave behind so it doesn't worry me; when my work is finished here I'll go. I'll give you a call when I'm done here. You might want to spend as much time with Linda as possible, Pastor; we leave early tomorrow morning."

"You were having a long chat with Johnny last night; it looked serious. Was it?"

61

"It was, Linda, and I need to talk to you about it. I should have spoken to you yesterday, but I didn't want to upset you."

"There's nothing that you could say or do that could upset me, Christian. Tell me."

"I have to go on a trip with Johnny, within the hour."

"Where are you going?"

"Jerusalem."

"Jerusalem, Christian! Can I come with you?"

"No, Linda. It's not a pleasure trip; I have to go without you. I know it's not great timing, but I have to go - it's an assignment from the Lord."

"The last time you went on a missions trip for the Lord it took over ten years for you to come back to me."

"It's not really a missions trip."

"Then what sort of trip is it? I have to know; tell me."

"I can't, Linda; I'm not too sure myself. All I know is that we have to put some discs into the mainframe of a super computer (how - I don't know; I'm trusting that Johnny will). I've no idea what's waiting for us, and that's why I have to tell you there might be a chance that we won't be coming back."

"What do you mean: *you might not be coming back?* You're worrying me now; how dangerous is this assignment, Christian?"

"Like I said, I don't know; I have to trust the Lord that, if I don't make it back, He will take care of you."

"Can't Johnny go on his own? I need you here with me."

"Sorry, Linda, I know it's something I have to do, and Johnny needs me with him."

"I need you, Christian. I need you. I'm not strong enough to lose you again."

"You're stronger than you think, Linda. When we pastored the church it was you who was there beside me, encouraging me. You were my rock - and still are. I know the Lord's will is for you to help these people while I'm away."

Linda sat down on the bed defeatedly. She knew once my mind was made up, there was no way I'd change it. "What about that walk you promised me?" she asked, and I could see she was holding back tears.

Sitting down on the bed beside her, I said, "I know I promised, Linda, but that was before I knew anything about this. If I come back we'll have that walk, and if not, when we get to Heaven I'll take you for a more wonderful walk that you could ever have here. So, one way or the other, I will keep my promise to you. I love you, Linda."

She blinked a tear away. "I love you too, and I'll keep you to that promise!"

We made our way out of our room to see all the others waiting for us.

"Pastor, I need your hand again - for the new identity chip: 'Robert Collins, State Communications Engineer.' I'm your colleague, 'Stephen Hammond, Senior State Engineer'."

"Am I going to have problems at the check-in desk with my ID not having the photo of the real person again?"

"Apparently not, it's all taken care of by your angel."

"How do you know that?"

"I like to say I know everything, but it was Mordecai who told me."

63

"And what's this 'senior' business?"

"Well it speaks for itself, Pastor; it's because I know more than you about communications," he said with a grin. "We have two hours to catch our flight."

Linda flung her arms around me; I knew by the tightness of her grip she didn't want to let me go. Seeing Johnny making his way to the door, I knew I had to pull myself away. Mark could see I needed help and came over. He put his arm around her.

"Don't worry, Pastor. She's in good company. You go and do what you have to do; we'll be here waiting for you when you return. May God go with you both."

"Take care of her, Mark."

6

"**H**ow long is this flight, Stephen?"

"About five hours. You might as well relax and enjoy the first-class facilities; we don't know what's waiting for us up ahead." Lowering his voice, he said, "Nice one with the name, . . . Robert. "

As I stared out of the plane window my thoughts were of Linda. It had been so hard leaving her. After a while I could feel my eyes starting to get heavy . . .

The next thing I knew, the stewardess was saying:

"Sirs, would you like something to eat?" She handed me the menu. Remembering what Johnny had said, and not knowing when we would eat again, I decided to have something that would see me through the day.

"How long have I been asleep, Stephen?

"Several hours, we should be landing soon. Past ... Robert."

Speaking quietly, I said: "Watch your words, Stephen. *Details*."

Chuckling, he said, "Nice one, Robert."

Still quietly, I asked, "So what's the plan when we land?"

"We make our way to the hotel, get some rest and then tomorrow we head for the Temple Mount."

"There's a guy across the aisle whose been watching us the whole time. Do you think we'll have anyone stopping us, asking questions?" I said softly.

"I've noticed him. O ye of little faith! Don't you know me yet? Why should we? We have top-level security passes; anyone would be insane to question them."

"Talk about blowing your own trumpet."

"Well, if you've got it, flaunt it, I say," he said, laughing.

"This is the Captain speaking; we'll be landing in Tel Aviv shortly. We hope you have enjoyed your flight. Please do not unfasten your seat belts until we have landed."

As we came out of Arrivals, a State guy met us.

"Sirs, your car is waiting outside to take you to the hotel, if you would follow me."

In the back of the car I asked Johnny, "Was the car you, or them?"

"Me of course," he said with a smug smile.

"Did you sleep well, Robert?"

"I must have been tired; I slept like a log. I normally don't sleep well in hotel beds."

"Eat up; we leave in half an hour. I'll meet you by the reception desk," he said getting up from the breakfast table.

"Do you always have to keep disappearing?" I called out to him. All that came back was his usual chuckle.

We walked through the revolving doors and out onto the street.

"I take it we know where we're going, Stephen?"

"To the old quarters of the city, not far from the Wall."

"I've always wanted to visit the Wall. I don't suppose we'll have time?"

"We'll be doing better than that. We'll be going down by its foundations. According to the instructions, there's a tunnel that's been excavated all along the Wall and, off the tunnel, is another one that leads to the Temple."

"I didn't see that."

"No, you wouldn't have. They only appeared this morning."

"*What*? That's amazing!"

"I guess it's because, if someone had got hold of the papers, they would know our mission. The information appears only when we need it."

"It sounds like you're used to it."

"You could say that. Don't forget, if anyone speaks to us, speak back with authority."

"I know, *authority*. By the way, I may be wrong but I'm sure that guy from the plane has been following us."

"I've been aware of him since we left the hotel; you're not wrong - it is the same guy. We need to lose him. There should be a market up ahead; I reckon we can lose him in the crowd."

As we quickened our pace, I asked Johnny if he had any idea who the guy might be.

"I'm not sure but he can't be anything to do with HQ Central; if he was he wouldn't be following us.

It's clear from our uniforms who we are and, as I said before, with our high clearance ID badges he would be foolish to question us, let alone follow us."

"Maybe we should stop him and ask who he is, you know - play the authority card."

"Not a bad idea, but we're on a tight schedule and it's critical we keep to it. No, we'll try to lose him."

Walking along the narrow streets, I couldn't help thinking that Jesus might have walked where I was treading. I could feel the ambience of the place, of centuries past, which would be impossible to imagine without being here. Johnny took us to a busy market and soon we were lost amongst the crowds.

"How far now, Stephen?"

"Not far," he said, looking at the paper.

Coming out of the market, I realised he was heading for a narrow, dark alley.

"I don't fancy going down there. Are you sure that's the way?"

"Sure it's the way. No need to be concerned; I know Mordecai is up ahead somewhere."

"Well that's okay then, no need to worry."

"It's true; he is."

Some distance into the alley, something made me turn around. My eyes caught the shape of a figure behind us but, in the blink of an eye, it had vanished. *But where to?* We hadn't passed any doors or pillars to hide behind. In the darkness I couldn't be sure if I was seeing things.

"Why are you stopping? Keep up."

Coming towards the end of the alley was a relief, but it wasn't to last.

Johnny stopped me before I could step out onto the street. "Can you see, across the road, the two armed guards at the entrance of that building?"

"Yeah."

"That's were we have to go. Inside the building are the steps to the tunnel. Don't forget, when we go over there, it's boldness and authority."

"I think I can manage that."

Johnny led the way, with me close behind him.

"Open up, trooper, we need entrance immediately," Johnny said, showing his ID.

The guard looked at our IDs and hastily unlocked the barred iron gate.

"Will you be long down there, Sir?"

"We wont be very long; there will be no need to re-lock the gate."

"But, Sir, we have our orders - to keep it locked at all times."

"Trooper, are you questioning my authority, because if you are I'll have you up before your superiors?"

"No, Sir," he said.

"Good, now get out of the way, and let us pass!"

Once inside the building, I followed Johnny down a flight of worn stone steps that took us to a subterranean passage.

"You might want to use your flashlight, but keep it on dim - we don't know who or what's down here."

I could see, by the huge, exposed stone blocks, that the tunnel was old, but not nearly as old as the Wall. "Are these blocks the foundations of the Wall?"

"By the size of them, I guess so. How they laid them is anyone's guess. Did you know that this stone here," he said pointing, "is the biggest stone in the Western Wall? It's often called the 'Western Stone' and ranks as one of the heaviest objects ever lifted by human beings without powered machinery. Its length is 13.6 metres."

"What's that in feet?" I asked, not really knowing much about metric measurements.

"About 45 ft, and the height is 3 metres - a few inches under 10 ft. It's been estimated that its width is between 3.5 metres and 4.5 metres (11 to 15 ft)."

'Very interesting," I commented, wanting to get on.

"Don't you want to know the weight of it?"

"Well, I suppose so."

"Well, if you're not that interested, I'll stop now."

"No, I am; I want to know. How heavy is it?"

"Its estimated weight is 520 metric tons."

"Where did you learn all this stuff?"

"It's a hobby of mine - Jewish history and archeology. There's more I could tell you, if you're interested."

"You might as well. I was going to ask how long it goes on for."

"It's about 1,591 ft, with parts of it so narrow that you can just squeeze through. I remember it from when I came here a long time ago."

"I suppose that's all stopped now?"

"That's right; it was when the New World Order took over. This place was too important to them. Tourists were the last things they wanted around here. There should be another tunnel about 150 feet ahead. It's been sealed off for hundreds of years, but it led to a small synagogue called 'The Cave', where the early Muslims allowed the Jews to pray in close proximity to the ruins of the Temple. But now the Jews can't get anywhere near it. I've a feeling the cave is where we've got to get to, being under the Temple.

"If the tunnel's blocked up, how are we going to get through it?"

"At this stage I don't know, but I'm sure we'll figure it out when we get there. Doesn't the good book say something like: 'I will show you a way where there is no way'?

Now where was I with the history lesson? Did you know that, from the time of King Solomon to the return from the Babylonian exile, the Temple Mount was a relatively small platform built on top of Mount Moriah? That was the site of the Temple. King Herod's greatest building project was . . . "

As I followed behind, listening to him pour out the history of the place, I was glad I didn't suffer from claustrophobia; the tunnel was not only dark, but narrow and dank. All the time we'd been walking, I had the same feeling I'd had before in the alley - of someone behind us.

There was one thing I didn't like, and it was not being in control of a situation. It felt like I was the hunted and I needed to turn the situation around and become the hunter. I turned off my flashlight to give me the advantage of surprise then I waited in the darkness, while Johnny prattled on ahead.

I had never experienced such thick darkness before but, being optimistic by nature, I knew I could use it to my advantage. I would wait for whoever it was to come to me; then I would find out why we were being followed.

It felt as though time had stopped; the only sound I could hear, apart from Johnny's distant voice somewhere ahead, was the sound of my heart beating fast. There was an eerie silence and yet I knew that whoever it was, was still coming my way.

I wanted to alert Johnny, but he was too far ahead to hear me, and it was obvious that he hadn't noticed that I had stopped, so I was alone to face what was coming. I could sense the humid atmosphere turning ice cold, and fear trying to take hold of me, as the unknown presence drew nearer.

"Move!" came the familiar voice in my head. Shaking off the fear, I turned on my flashlight so I could see ahead of me, but I couldn't resist shining it down the tunnel to see whomever it was that was following.

As I did, the beam caught the face of what I could only describe as something not human. I had never seen a demon before, but this could be nothing else - a face I would never forget. Considering I had not walked or run in twelve years, my therapy was now being put to the test. I ran down that tunnel at a speed that would have beaten all records.

"Johnny, where are you?" I cried out as I ran. When I stopped to get my breath, a hand grabbed my shoulder from behind.

"Where did you get to? I suddenly realised I had been talking to myself. Why were you running?"

Still trying to get my breath, I panted: "Don't do that, Johnny! I've had enough scary moments down here."

"What's spooked you? You look as if you've had a fright," he said, shining his light in my face.

"You could say that again," I said, taking a deep breath. I think we should get out of here - like *now.* But not the way we've just come."

"Take another deep breath, Pastor. We have a job to do and, even if I agreed with you, there's no other way out. So what happened?"

"You're right - we have to go on. It's nothing, probably just my imagination running wild. Let's get going. Which way then?"

"This off-shoot corridor behind me. I reckon it's the one I was talking about; you can see it's been unblocked. I've already been a way down it, then I noticed you weren't behind me. Further on, it looks as if there's been a lot of new construction. I'm not rushing you but, as I said, it's all about time; so if you've got your breath let's press on."

As I followed Johnny I couldn't help looking behind. I couldn't see anything but I couldn't shake off the feeling that something was still following us.

We came to a halt; a locked iron-barred door blocked our way.

"Now what, Johnny?"

"No problem, Pastor," he said, producing a device from his bag.

The lock made a buzz and the door sprang open. We hadn't walked far before we were stopped again by another door. Again Johnny produced the device, making the door open.

I said, "What's with all these doors?" and we soon came across a third. "At this rate you might as well keep the device in your hand, I shouldn't think this is the last."

"You could be right. What the . . .?"

73

The clanging sound of the doors behind slamming shut made the pair of us look at each other in dismay.

"Sounds as if we have company, Pastor. Whoever that was, is telling me they have no intention of letting us leave. I deliberately left them open so we would have a quick get-away."

"What do we do now?"

"We keep going."

As we made our way further along, sure enough, there was another door. Johnny quickly made it open, in spite of each door having a different code.

We heard another clang, a pause and then a further clang; it was the sound of two more doors being shut behind us.

"By the sound of it, whoever it is has increased their pace."

"What are you doing, Johnny?"

"I'm locking the door; hopefully it will stop whoever it is following us."

"But it means we're locked in," I protested.

"What choice do we have? It's either that or maybe being caught. The objective is to get done what we have been sent to do. The worst that can happen is, we die."

"If you don't mind, Johnny, I don't want to think about that. I really would like to get back to Linda."

We picked up our pace and headed down the tunnel.

"Not again! How many doors are there?"

"Let's keep going, Pastor."

I couldn't help thinking that whatever was behind me earlier was still following us. In fact, right from the start of the plane flight, it was as if somehow someone knew about our mission. The face on the plane had looked human, but the face I had glimpsed in the tunnel certainly wasn't.

"I reckon this is the last one."

"How do you know?"

"The door is solid steel. I think the computer is behind this door, and if it is, that makes us directly under the Temple."

Johnny was pointing the device at the door and punching in different codes, but the door wasn't opening.

"Problem?"

"I wouldn't say a problem, Pastor; just a little setback."

"Well, whatever the 'little setback' is, we haven't got long before our guest is with us," I said looking back down the tunnel.

Clang!

"Your locked door didn't stop him; we need that door opened *now* Johnny!"

In the darkness, my flashlight picked up a figure making its way towards us, while Johnny was struggling to make the door open.

"Pray!" came that familiar voice.

"Johnny, can I take over?"

"What are you going to do, Pastor, pray?"

"Exactly that."

"You might not want to touch the door, Pastor. I don't know what's going on the other side, but it feels quite hot."

I put my hand towards the door, making sure I didn't touch it, and said, "Lord you have authority over the Earth. You gave that authority to your servant, Moses, to part the Red Sea when the Egyptians were following. Now I'm asking that you

75

demonstrate that same power and open this door and save us. Amen."

A shaky "Amen", came from Johnny, who was behind me facing the figure, which was only a short distance away.

"Now, Lord, would be a good time!" I said with my back to the door seeing what Johnny was seeing, "please!"

7

A sudden flash of bright light came between the figure and us. I had never witnessed the supernatural before, but before us materialised a huge man in golden armour, with an outline glowing in radiant light. As one of his hands was held outstretched towards the dark figure and the other towards us, the door sprang open.

"Nice to see you, Johnny. If you and the Pastor wouldn't mind stepping through the door to do what you have to do, I have a little work here."

"*Mordecai?* Is that you?" Johnny said with a look of relief on his face.

"I said I would be with you; now **go!**"

As soon as Johnny and I entered, the door closed behind us with a metallic clang. We didn't need our flashlight, as the room was lit up with a red light. We were in a huge cave, and in the middle was what we assumed must be the computer, although not like any computer we had seen before.

Apart from its size, which was dwarfing us, it was surrounded by large fiery rings, which were generating the heat in the room and causing the

77

steel door to be so hot. Each ring was pulsating upwards, outside a large diameter transparent shaft mounted on top of the computer. They were passing through the chamber roof and back down again to repeat the process over and over. I assumed they were going in and out of the Temple above. It was obvious that this computer was far ahead of our technology.

Then, as if the computer had sensed our presence, it let out a high-pitched, piercing hum, causing us to slap our hands over our ears. We stood by the door, hoping that the shrill noise would subside, but the computer increased its defence with the fiery rings changing from red to blue, increasing the temperature in the room.

Even though the noise in the chamber was loud, the noise outside the door was even louder. It was something my ears had never heard before – a cross between groaning and screaming. From under the door there seemed to come flashes of intense light, like lightening but much brighter.

Although Mordecai was strong he could sense that this wouldn't be over quickly. He had fought many battles over the years, but this one was different. Every time his flashing sword struck the figure, making it fall to the ground, two more figures materialised. He had an onslaught both from his left and his right. With a sweeping slash from his sword, the two figures fell to the ground.

There was a pause from the attacks, but Mordecai knew it wasn't over. He had been around for a long time and was a warrior trained in spiritual warfare. He knew that what had just come at him was merely fodder, sent to evaluate his strength.

But he was ready for whatever the evil force was going to throw at him; he knew the next onslaught would be big. Waiting for it to happen, he was aware that this was a tactic of the enemy, aimed at causing him to relax his guard. But the waiting game was what he excelled in.

In the Great Hall where he trained, he would be standing alone in the middle of the hall with his eyes shut. Then, without warning, a virtual figure would come out of nowhere to attack him. With his senses highly tuned, he would strike with his sword and destroy the figure. Every day the numbers and speed of those coming at him would increase. When he had reached his target of destroying a hundred, he knew he would make the grade of Second in Command. And now his training was to be put to the test. But this was no virtual game, for this was only too real.

With his back a short distance from the cave door, ready with sword in hand, he closed his eyes to sharpen his other senses. As fast as Mordecai was, he wasn't fast enough to sense one of them behind him. Without warning, he felt a thrust of white-hot steel pierce his armour and enter his flesh, distracting him from the new figures appearing in front of him.

He reached behind him and pulled out a twisted steel lance from his back; almost at the same time he thrust his sword into the figures in front. The figure behind threw itself onto his back, slashing away with its razor sharp claws. With one hand he grabbed the figure and threw it to the ground and, with its own lance, Mordecai ran it through.

The figures now were multiplying, filling the corridor in front of him. He knew, at all costs, he had to hold them off from reaching the door. As powerful and skilled as he was, he had never fought so many at one time. Row after row of them filled the tunnel. The sound of steel clashing from sword to lances filled the place. Fiery arrows were raining down at Mordecai, with many piercing his amour.

Despite his valiant fighting, Mordecai realised he was being overwhelmed. He could feel himself being forced to the ground by the sheer volume and weight of his opponents, who were now all over him, thrusting their weapons into him. Even those who did not have a weapon were clawing and slashing at him with their razor-sharp claws, wanting a piece of him for a trophy.

Mordecai could feel the power leaving him, and his only thought was that he had failed the assignment, and let Michael down. He had just about resigned himself to his fate, when he felt the weight on top of him lighten. The figures were flying off him, crashing into the ceiling and walls.

"I thought you could do with a little help here, Mordecai."

"Aquila! You took your time!"

"I didn't want to spoil it for you. I could see you were trying to enjoy yourself, but by the state of you, apparently not," she said, pulling arrows from his armour.

"I had it under control," he said as he lay there.

"Yeah, sure," Aquila smiled, "so are you going to get up, or have I got to do the job of disposing of this lot for you?"

Mordecai sprang to his feet and joined Aquila in finishing them off.

Because of the noise from the computer, we had to shout at each other.

"I think your Mordecai's having some sort of battle out there," I said.

"Let's hope he wins then, Pastor, for our sake," he shouted back.

"You say 'hope', and he's your angel. Where's your faith? Of course he will!"

"Thanks, Pastor. I needed that. In the face of adversity, it's so easy to let slip. It tests your faith, don't you think?"

"That's what adversity's for – to build our faith. We'd better get on. So do you know how and where to put the discs into that thing with that amount of heat surrounding it?"

"Not at the moment; it's not until now that we need to know."

Johnny took out the instructions from his pocket, and in front of our eyes the words appeared on the paper, showing how and where to insert the discs. But we could see other words appearing, which drew our attention.

'Take up the shield of faith, with which you can extinguish all the flaming arrows of the evil one.'

'I did not give you a spirit of fear, but of power and of love and of a sound mind.'

"God has given us scriptures, Pastor."

"It's His Rhema Word – to empower us. Faith is going to get us through this. Fear is the enemy of faith; don't let it get to you."

We were still several paces from the rings and, even at that distance, the heat was starting to scorch our clothes. We were faced with a choice: if we took our hands away from our ears the effect of the piercing hum would deafen us (or worse, damage our brains), and if we didn't, the heat would blister our faces.

We had no option but to turn and slowly walk backwards towards the fiery rings, which had started darting out towards us. I went first, with Johnny closely following me. Apart from the intense heat and the smell of scorched clothing, a tangible menace was radiating from them; the closer we got, the more fear tried to penetrate us.

"I think we should pray the scriptures, Pastor. This must be some sort of defence mechanism."

"Lord, thank you for the scriptures. We now claim your Word. (Declare them with me Johnny). "No evil . . . " was all I could manage. The rest was stopped short by the fiery rings speeding up, turning from blue to white and omitting a higher pitched hum that was drowning out my words.

"Keep going, Pastor!" Johnny shouted.

"What are you doing, Johnny?" I cried out as he stepped between me and the rings.

"Say them now, Pas ----- tor!"

I knew I had to declare the Word, but I was torn between that and dragging Johnny out of the way. I could see he was on the verge of passing out from the heat and I didn't know if the force of the rings would kill him or have some irreversible effect on him.

Because of Johnny shielding me with his body, I could feel the heat and fear weakening. I started to speak out the scriptures and, as I finished declaring them, the pulsating fiery rings and the high-pitched hum suddenly stopped. The room became dark, so I turned on my flashlight to see that Johnny was just about to collapse. I rushed forward in time to stop him from falling to the ground.

"Speak to me, Johnny! Say something," I implored as I held him under the arms and lowered him to the floor.

Opening his eyes, he said, "Did we do it, Pastor?"

"Yes, we did it. Thanks to you, Johnny. What made you do that? How do you feel?"

"Give me a moment and I'll be with you."

I watched him slowly stand and, before my eyes, I could see the blisters on his back and his burnt clothes returning to normal.

With words that could only have come from him, he said, "I stepped out in faith, knowing that He had taken me this far and He wasn't going to desert me now. Yeah, I feel fine. You can't keep a good man down, Pastor," he chuckled.

"Yeah, I can see that you're back to your normal self."

"Okay, let's get these discs in and get out of here, Pastor."

Johnny took the sapphire discs out of their pouch and laid them in the palm of his hand. As he walked towards the computer, a small sliding hatch opened.

"I guess they're meant to go in there," he said, placing them into the opening.

"I think we'd better retreat towards the door, Johnny; we're dealing with the unknown here."

"Amen to that, Pastor," he said following me.

We shone our flashlights towards the computer and waited. Suddenly there was a quiet hum, followed by a flicker of light, which turned into a ring of pure white light that went up the shaft. Within seconds, rings of light were flashing at a great speed, travelling up and down the shaft. The hum turned into precise, clear words.

"Are you hearing what I'm hearing, Pastor?"

"I sure am, Johnny. They are the words of God, and they're doing what Mordecai said they would do."

The light was so beautiful we didn't want to take our eyes from it but I said. "Let's go Johnny - we've done what we were sent to do."

We made our way towards the door and Johnny pointed his device at it.

"There's a small problem, Pastor. The door won't open. I think Mordecai locked it and, as much as I hope he's dealt with what was on the other side, I can't be sure if there's something waiting for us."

"At the moment, let's just worry about how we get out of here."

"Mordecai, are you out there? We need a little help here!" he shouted out.

As we waited, I asked, "Does Mordecai look how you thought he would?"

"I often wondered what he would look like if he revealed himself, and he's *nothing* like I expected."

"So what did you expect?"

"Sort of more like us. Human. Not that big and awesome."

"Well, he is from the supernatural realm, Johnny."

"Have you ever seen a supernatural being, Pastor?"

"No, unless Smiley is one, then yes. But she did look human (and pretty with it)."

"Maybe they can take on human forms."

84

"You know, Johnny, it says in the Bible, in fact I think it's in Hebrews, that some have entertained angels without knowing it, and for us to do that they must look human.

Suddenly they heard Mordecai's voice: "Give me a minute – I'm just finishing up out here!"

The door gave a click and opened on it's own. We stepped out expecting a dark corridor but, to our amazement, it was glowing with warm light. As far as we could see down the corridor, the floor was littered with burnt corpses.

At the end of the corridor stood two huge figures, one male and one female, wearing golden amour. As far as I could make out, the male was the same figure that Johnny called Mordecai, but the other I hadn't seen before. We stood there mesmerised by the awesome sight of them, Mordecai leaning on his sword, and the woman holding a golden staff in front of her.

"By the sound of His Words filling the air, I take it you two achieved your mission?" Mordecai said in a deep powerful voice, stepping to one side to let us pass.

"I believe so," Johnny replied.

"Hello, Christian. We meet again," said the female, smiling."

I immediately recognised the voice, "*Smiley*?"

"Yes, but it's Aquila. I'm your angel, Christian, assigned to look after you."

I had never spoken to an angel before, and I found myself saying, "You'll always be 'Smiley' to me."

She didn't say anything but gave me one of her reassuring smiles.

"His Word is causing chaos out there, Johnny," said Mordecai.

"His Word is truth. It will not return empty, but will accomplish what He wants and achieve the purpose for which it was sent. The heavens declare the glory of God; the skies proclaim the works of His hands. Day after day they pour forth speech; night after night they display knowledge. There is no speech or language where His voice is not heard. His voice goes out into all the Earth, His Words to the end of the world," declared Aquila.

As she spoke the Words of God, the anointing from them was so strong we had a job to stand.

"You must change your IDs; they will be looking for you. Give me your hands."

As we held out our hands, Mordecai touched them with his huge finger. I could feel a power I'd never experienced before coming into my being.

"There, new IDs. You are State Security Officials now. You must go."

By the time we made it half way up the steps, I felt I just had to turn around to view once more the awesome sight of two angels, but to my disappointment they had disappeared.

Walking through the building towards the entrance, we were glad to see that the two guards had gone. I could see what Mordecai meant by 'chaos'; people everywhere were running around with their hands on their ears, some crouching on the ground, not able to block out the penetrating Word of God that was filling the airways.

We had just made it to the other side of the road, when we heard the screeching tyres of a van pulling up outside the entrance of the tunnel. The back doors flew open and a large number of troupers rushed out and poured down into the tunnel.

"Excellent timing on my part, don't you think, Pastor?"

"What do you mean, *your* part? You had nothing to do with it."

Our banter was stopped short by a voice:

"You two!"

It came from the open window of a State car that pulled up alongside us.

"Anything to report?"

"Not yet, Sir," Johnny answered.

"Keep your eyes open. They couldn't have got far; the city is on lock-down. The Supreme One wants them apprehended before nightfall."

"Yes, Sir!"

As they drove off, Johnny turned and said chuckling, "He's got no chance."

"Where to now, J . . ." I stopped myself short, knowing there were ears everywhere, human and otherwise. "Do we have new ID names?" I whispered."

"I wouldn't have thought so - just a number. I'll let you know what they are as soon as I find a quiet spot."

It wasn't long before we found the doorway of a disused shop.

"In here," he said, pulling me by the arm. "Hand!"

He took out his ID implant and scanner. "CCG-1987. Memorise it, in case you're asked for it."

"That shouldn't be a problem, it's my initials and date of birth."

"What does the other C stand for?"

"Charles. Wow! My memory's back to normal."

"Your parents chose quite a posh name," he said with his usual chuckle, which was beginning to grate a little.

"Well at least I have a real name," I countered.

"Touché, Charles."

"So what's your number?"

Scanning his hand, he answered: "JG -1980."

"Mordecai's made it easy for us to remember, but won't my ID cause a problem if it's scanned, since my name isn't on the system?"

"Mordecai wouldn't have given it to you if it would. Trust him, Charles."

"Stop calling me that. We're supposed to be using our numbers."

"Just trying to lighten the atmosphere."

"*Don't!*"

"Don't what?"

"I thought you were going to finish with your annoying chuckle."

"Annoying is it?" he said going quiet.

Seeing that I had upset him, I said, "Well just a bit. No, it's not too bad. You carry on; it wouldn't be you if you didn't."

With his face lightening up, he let out a chuckle and said, "Well, if you insist."

Giving up and shaking my head, I said, "Let's go."

"Sir, I don't know if you can hear us above this noise, but we're approaching the main chamber; do we enter?"

"Any sign of the intruders?" came back a voice amid a lot of static on the radio.

"No, Sir; not in the tunnels. The chamber door is closed; there's a chance they're still inside. Your instructions, Sir?' There was no answer. "Sir, your instructions?"

"If you can hear me, proceed with caution. Do not kill the intruders. The Supreme One wants them for questioning. But you are, at all costs, to de-activate the device that has been planted. Do you understand, trooper, *at all costs*? The door will be opened for you."

The officer in charge asked, "Did you make out what the orders were?"

"All I could make out, Sir, was: 'You are, at all costs, to de-activate the device that's been planted' and something about the door."

The door gave a click. "In you go!" commanded the senior officer. The second in command, seeing that there was nobody in the room, said, "All clear, Sir."

The senior officer and team of engineers entered and made their way to the computer. The blue sapphire discs could be clearly seen spinning, radiating the rings of pure light up and down the shaft.

"I've never seen anything like it, Sir. How do we go about de-activating it?" shouted the chief engineer to the superior.

"I guess you go and remove it with your hands, man," he shouted back, hardly able to hear because of God's word filling the room.

The engineer nodded at a colleague, who proceeded nervously towards the sapphires, while the superior cautiously stepped back towards the door.

With droplets of sweat glistening on his brow, the engineer gingerly touched one of the rings. Instantly intense rays of white light shot out towards every man in the room, vapourising them.

"Officer Shorts here. Trooper! Report to me! Why can I still hear these *words*?"

There was no answer. "Trooper, speak to me! Is anyone there?"

8

"**D**o you know where you're going, JG?"

"Not far from here. In the Jewish quarters are people that will help us; they have a safe house - we're heading there."

"That suits me. With the amount of activity of the State police, the quicker we get off these streets the better."

Although we had confidence in our State uniforms, I could see that Johnny was playing it safe by taking the back streets and alleys as much as he could. We had just come out of an alley onto a main street where there were several troopers being given instructions by a high-ranking officer. The scene was almost comical. Standing there, barking at these tall guards was the officer, half the size of them. We quickened our pace and started to walk past them, when a loud voice roared:

"You two!" It was the voice of the short officer.

"Keep walking; pretend we didn't hear him."

"You two! Stop!"

"What do we do?"

"We stop; we can't outrun bullets."

91

Turning to face him, Johnny said, "Sorry Sir, we didn't hear you with all the noise going on."

"That's my question! Why haven't you got your ear defenders on?"

"Because, when we left for our assignment, this offensive noise wasn't being broadcasted, so we had no reason to take them with us, Sir," Johnny said.

"You're right there, man, about it being offensive." He nodded towards the ensigns on our uniforms. "I see that you're Security. What division are you from?"

"Northern Division, Sir."

"You're a long way from there. So what brings you into my division? I haven't requested any outside security, or been informed of any security breaches."

"We have been sent to help you track the saboteurs that are responsible for this, Sir."

"But you said that you were assigned before this dirge was being broadcasted, in which case you wouldn't have known about any intruders. Who did you say was your senior officer? "

Knowing Johnny had to think quickly to cover his slip, I couldn't help thinking, *details Johnny, details! Whatever you say, please get it right.*

"I didn't, sir."

"So who is it?" he said with a tone of suspicion and flexing his cane.

"Commander Rav Nagad, Sir."

Lord I hope he's real and you gave Johnny that name, I prayed silently.

"Nagad you say? I know him quite well."

Thank you, Lord! I released the breath I'd been holding. Thinking that he was satisfied with the answer, we started to walk off.

"Hold fast you two. You, man with the reader, bring that over here!" he bellowed. Now, let's see who we have here. Hands!"

Johnny went first. There was a pause, and then the guy with the reader said, "JG1980 State Security, Northern District, Sir."

Knowing that my details were not on the system, I feared the game would be up for us, or at least me. I pleaded under my breath: *Smiley, if you're there I need you – right now.*

I'm here. Trust me. It was as though those words of assurance were whispered in my ear.

"Hand, man!" The officer bellowed at me. I walked forward and held out my hand. Just as the scanner's beam was about to read my details, there was the sound of distant rumbling and we could feel vibration beneath our feet. Before we knew what was happening, the ground shook violently and a large fissure opened in the road a little way from us. It tracked its way down the main street with buildings crashing to the ground all around us.

"Earthquake, Sir!" came a panic-stricken voice from one of the men. But the officer was already on his way to his car, speeding away from the fissure that was pursuing close behind him. The men ran in the opposite direction trying to escape.

"Thanks, Smiley," I called out. **You're welcome,** came back.

"What was that all about, CG?"

"Trust, JG, trust. I think that's our cue to get out of here."

Because of the chaos brought on by the earthquake we were able to make our way through the streets without any fear of being stopped.

"So this 'Rav Nagad', do you know him?"

93

"No, the name just popped into my head."

"The Lord's so faithful. I prayed that he would give you a real name."

"And I thought it was me - with my brilliant mind," he replied with a little chuckle.

"I think not."

"That earthquake was incredible. Although the buildings were coming down all around us, not one bit of debris touched us. Do you think that guy in the car made it?"

"I don't know, CG, but that fissure was pretty close behind him."

"I hope you repented for calling God's Word offensive. Couldn't you have chosen another word?"

"A play on words, old chap. I meant 'on the attack' but I knew how he would take it."

"Okay, I'll let you have that one."

"Good, Pastor, can we get on now?"

We had walked past several blocks of rubble, when we saw the senior officer's State car. The crushed rear end was sticking out of the fissure in what was left of the road.

"There's your answer, CG. I don't think we'll have any more problems with *him*."

"I hope the airport wasn't affected; we'll need it operational to get out of here."

"The quake was quite big, but hopefully not too big to keep us from leaving. We'll find out tomorrow, but first the safe house, which shouldn't be too far now."

"How do you know it didn't get destroyed in the quake?"

"It wouldn't be called a 'safe house', now would it?" he said, with another chuckle.

Humouring him, I replied, "Of course it wouldn't."

The quake had destroyed much of the block, leaving it like a war zone, yet I could see he still knew where he was going as we ventured through what was left of the side streets. The air was filled with the sound of screaming people running from the buildings into the street in fear of an aftershock, and the Word of God could still be heard above it all.

The devastation seemed to go on forever, but as we entered into a new area I could see that there were a few houses still standing.

"What you reckon? Do you think the people who live in them know the Lord?"

"Hard to say, CG, it would be nice to think so, but it could be just luck on their part."

"So are we there yet?

"I can't believe you just said that."

"Said what?"

"Are we there yet? You sounded just like a kid in the back of a car. Are we there yet!"

"Very funny. I was just enquiring how much further we had to go?"

"Joking aside, I can't count the number of times people back home have said to me, 'Do you think we're there yet?'"

"And what did you tell them?"

Speaking very quietly, he said: "I could only tell them what they wanted to hear; that by the way things are and by the signs, that we were very near. Every day they prayed that He would come and take them. But now they've got a Pas... I mean Leader, it has given them hope to carry on."

"I will do my best. By the way, why are we whispering? Surely they can't hear what we're saying now - with the Word filling the air?"

"It's better to be cautious, CG. I know from past experience that certain key words automatically set off alarms in the system. I don't think I have to tell you what they are. Do I?"

"Now you've explained, no."

Walking on a little further, he said "And the answer to your question is . . . there."

Between two intact buildings was the entrance to a bazaar, which would normally be busy with people, but because of the quake, it was now deserted. It was obvious that they'd left in a hurry as there were overturned tables and merchandise strewn across the narrow, cobbled alleyway. Picking our way over it, I followed Johnny, who stopped at a small shop that sold drapes.

"This is it," he said.

"But it's a shop?" I replied.

He merely smiled and walked in, leaving me standing at the entrance. He went to the back, slipped between the heavy drapes and disappeared.

Forgetting myself, I called out, "Johnny!"

"A head appeared between the drapes and said, "You coming?"

Behind the drapes was a steel door, above which I could see a small camera. By its movement I could tell it was monitoring us. Johnny looked up at the camera and said, "Manoach, my brother."

There was a buzz, then the door clicked and opened.

"Yitzhak! Shalom, my brother. It's been a long time. Has the Lord been good to you?" said a long-haired, bearded man. His embrace of Johnny seemed to go on forever.

When they eventually finished embracing, Johnny replied, "Yes, He has poured out blessing after blessing. And you, my brother?"

"He's been good - blessing me with strays. So tell me, Yitzhak, what brings you here? You wouldn't happen to have anything to do with this wonderful event of God's Word filling the air, would you?"

"No, Manoach; only God could do that. He might have used the Pastor here, and me, to help Him a little but we're just His servants."

"Azriel שמות שלך צריכה להיות," Manoach said.

I whispered in Johnny's ear, "What did he say?"

"He said our names should be Azriel,"

"What does that mean?" I asked.

"Helpers of God. Sorry, Pastor, you must excuse me; I should have introduced you. Manoach, this is Pastor and friend, Christian Goodfellow."

"Shalom, Pastor Christian Goodfellow."

"Please, call me Christian; we're all equal in the eyes of God."

"True, my friend. My home is your home; now come, let's eat - for it is a day to celebrate the goodness of the Lord, that He has brought you into my home. Come!"

We followed him into another room.

"Freida! We have guests! Prepare some food and drink; they have come a long way," he called.

A woman came into the room, smiling. She reminded me of Linda when she was younger, with her hair tied up under a headscarf.

"Freida, this is Pastor Christian."

"Shalom, Pastor Christian."

"And I don't have to tell you who this is," Manoach said.

"It's been too long, Yitzhak! We have missed your company," she said hugging Johnny. "You look thin in the face; you need a good woman to look after you," she said, squeezing his cheeks.

"Leave him alone, woman. He has all he needs; he has God with him. Now if you get us some food, you might be able to fill his cheeks out a bit."

Johnny let out one of his chuckles. "It's great seeing you again, Freida. After all these years you're still the young beauty I remember. I don't know how you ended up with an old man like Manoach, here. You should have chosen a younger one."

Smiling, she fluttered her eyelids and went off to the kitchen.

"It appears that you have learnt to laugh at last, Yitzhak. You were always too serious. Sit, sit, we have much catching up to do. Tell me, how are things in England? We don't get much information here; only what they want us to hear," said Manoach.

"About the same as here; there are eyes and ears everywhere. Times are getting darker."

Interrupting Johnny, I said, "But His grace is causing the light to get lighter."

"How true, Pastor Christian," Manoach replied.

"Just Christian," I reminded him.

Johnny lent over and said to me, "He's a man with great respect for your title, Pastor." Turning to Manoach, he said: "We heard back home that it's a tinder box out here."

"True, Yitzhak; riots, and raids on people's homes, installing cameras, as well as the impact of the 'chips'. And, before you ask Pastor, we're safe here from all that. It's an every-day event to hear rumours of other nations planning to wipe us off the face of the earth, and the so-called 'Supreme Ruler' living in the temple is encouraging it all. But then, what would you expect from the Antichrist? If it wasn't for our faith, our hearts would fail."

"The Bible spoke of this long ago. Now we're living in that time."

"Yes, Pastor, we are. So, how long will you be staying?"

"Over night if that's okay. Our flight leaves tomorrow evening, but we need things to die down a bit before we make our way to the airport."

"I take it by that you mean the security people are searching for you? Do they know who you are?"

"Sort of. If it hadn't been for the earthquake I don't think we would be here."

"Yes, that was sudden. The moment we felt the tremor, Freida and I prayed."

"You can thank the Pastor for that," Johnny said, looking at me.

"Needs must, Johnny," I replied.

"Yes, but an earthquake was a bit extreme. If they did scan your ID they wouldn't have seen that it wasn't your face on it."

"Look, who am I to question an angel?"

"Do you two always carry on like this?" Manoach asked.

"Put it this way, Manoach, it's never serious; we have a good laugh together," Johnny said.

"So tonight we'll pray that He will protect you," Manoach announced.

Seeing that Freida had laid the table with food, Manoach said, "Come now, let's give thanks and eat."

Lying on the makeshift beds that Freida had prepared for us, I asked: "So, Johnny, why does he call you Yitzhak?"

"Because it is my name."

"You're Jewish?"

"Yes, I moved to England some fifteen years ago. I used to come back here twice a year, but I haven't returned since all the travel restrictions were put in place."

"So how do you know him?"

"He's my brother."

"We're all brothers in Christ, aren't we?"

"Yes, but he really is my brother."

"I wouldn't have known it - you look so different."

"Yes, I was always the better-looking one," he said as he let out one of his annoying chuckles.

"If you say so, Johnny, or do I call you Yitzhak while we're here?"

"Just Johnny will do."

"So how did you end up with the name Johnny?"

"It didn't start off as Johnny. When I moved to England I decided it would be safer to change my name to Edward Smith, it was as English as I could think of, what with all the anti-Semitism. Do you remember I told you I had to erase my details from the system when I left the I.T Company, and I made 'Johnny Gold' my new name?"

"I think so. So you're really 'Yitzhak'. Yitzhak what?"

"Goldstein. Yitzhak Jonathan Goldstein."

"I was going to ask how you understood Hebrew, but that explains it. By the way I know all Jewish names have a meaning. What does Yitzhak mean?"

"It means: 'He will laugh'," he said sleepily.

"Well, your parents sure gave you the right name, and what about Manoach?"

"It means, 'resting place'."

"Hence the safe house?"

"You know, Pastor, I never thought of that. It looks like God had a purpose for us from the start," he said, yawning.

"He had it all worked out, even before we were born. So what's the plan for tomorrow, Johnny?"

There was no answer. I could see he was already asleep.

I woke to the aroma of coffee and cooking. I could see Johnny's bed was empty but his distinctive chuckle from the other room told me where he was. Entering, I could see the three of them sitting around the table and   wished them good morning.

"Boker tov, Pastor, boker tov," chorused Manoach and Freida.

Johnny smiled, "They said 'Good morning'."

"Coffee with your breakfast, Pastor?"

"Yes please, Freida. I'm sure it was the aroma of your coffee and cooking that woke me up."

"As you're leaving us today, I thought I'd cook you our traditional Passover breakfast, Matzo Brei."

"This looks wonderful, Freida. I recognize the egg, but tell me what's this?"

"Crumbled matzo; it's made of plain white flour and water. It is the substitute for bread during Passover, a holiday in which Jews refrain from eating bread, leavened products, or the five grains

101

known as barley, spelt, rye, oats, and wheat in any processed form."

"Freida! I don't think the Pastor needs a lesson in Jewish cookery and culture."

"No, that's okay Manoach; I find it interesting. It's not Passover at the moment is it?"

"Oh no, Pastor. I just thought it would be nice to do something special. Now eat," she ordered.

"Well that was delicious, Freida."

"So, Pastor, I was saying to Yitzhak, it's gone crazy out there. The police are stopping everyone - searching for you two, but the plus side is that God's Word can still be heard everywhere. People are covering their ears or wearing ear defenders and I noticed that those who weren't were being stopped."

"That reminds me, do you have any around Manoach? It was not wearing them that got us noticed."

"You underestimate me, little brother. Of course I do; how many pairs do you want?"

"Just hand over the muffs."

Manoach went off to another room and returned with two pairs of new defenders.

"How did you get hold of those?"

"It's *who* you know little brother."

"Are they kosher - official police ones with the built in radio?"

"Of course."

"Now I know where you get it from, Johnny," I couldn't resist saying.

"Well, it doesn't matter if we're caught. His will has been done and that's all that counts."

"I don't think the Lord's finished with you two yet, Yitzhak."

"Amen there, Manoach," I added. "I've a lovely wife and I made her a promise I'd be back, and with the Lord's help I will."

"Well, Manoach, my brother, it's time that the Pastor and I made a move. Till we meet again, my brother,
Freida. Shalom."

"Shalom, my brother. May the Lord go with you both."

We set off, not knowing what was waiting for us, but Manoach was right - we had the assurance that God was with us.

9

As we emerged from the bazaar onto the street, I could see what Manoach meant by things 'going crazy'. The place was swarming with police. In desperation they were herding those who didn't have their ears covered into large police vans and driving off with them. Their fate didn't take any brains to work out, having seen the holding pens myself.

To avoid the crowds, we tried to keep to the side streets as much as possible. Unexpectedly, we came across a group of people not trying to protect their ears, and, by the look on their faces, I could see how fearful they were of us. As we walked on by without saying a word, a voice called out from behind us.

"You two, stop!"

Not again! I knew from the sound and authority in the voice that it was the small officer. We slowly turned around to see the little guy standing there, shining with his own importance, dressed in State uniform and accompanied by several others that dwarfed him. They had surrounded the group of people.

105

"Why didn't you interrogate these people?" He demanded, looking up at Johnny.

"They didn't look the sort to have been involved, Sir. We had no reason to suspect them."

"What do you mean by that? Everyone who's not trying to block out this noise is a suspect, even those who are in uniform. Your orders were to stop everyone . . ." he said pausing.   I could see him looking at Johnny's ID badge.

"JG 1980. Your ID indicates that you're from the Northern Sector. What are you doing here? Wait a minute! You're the two I saw earlier."

Oh no - not again. I thought we'd seen the last of him back there in that quake. Will he remember he was about to scan my ID?

"Pastor, be ready to run. Keep an eye on my lead," Johnny whispered.

The little guy came strutting over to Johnny and proceeded to tap on his ID badge with his cane. The rest of the men followed and were standing close behind him.

"I am waiting for an answer, man!" he said, continuing to tap.

The next thing I knew, Johnny had picked the little guy up by his lapels and heaved him backwards onto the men.

"Run!" Johnny said.

As I ran up the street, I turned to see the little guy and the men getting up on their feet.

"Shoot them! Shoot them!" he yelled at the top of his voice.

I heard a volley of gunshots break out. With nowhere to turn left or right, I expected to feel the impact of the bullets, but somehow we were still running as the men kept firing. Mystified that we reached the end of the street alive, I had to stop and turn to see why.

Immediately I could see the reason those bullets hadn't touched us. Standing there with their backs to us were Mordecai and Aquila. They were taking the impact of the shots; I could see on the floor all around them were scattered bullets. It was as if the bullets were hitting a brick wall.

"Are you seeing this, Johnny? It's so awesome!" I called out to him.

Johnny came back to join me. "They're good aren't they? That will teach you to mess with Johnny Gold!" he shouted to the little guy.

Aquila turned, smiled and gestured with her hand to go.

"I think that's our cue to leave, Johnny."

As we left I added: "I don't think you should have told him your name."

"Maybe not, but it felt good at the time."

"Sir, whatever they are, our weapons have no effect on them."

"Hold your position," the little guy commanded as he ran off in the opposite direction.

The two angels moved towards the troopers, who were still firing their weapons.

A flash of light came out of the street followed by "Arrrh!"

"That didn't sound too good, Johnny."

"What person in their right mind would just stand there firing at two mighty angels? They got what they deserved. We'd better go back to not using our names when we get onto the main street. I'm not

107

sure if the listening points were knocked out in the quake."

"Sure. How far to the airport?"

"About five miles. Providing we don't have any more hassle from jumped up little squirts, we should be there soon."

"Do you think they know we're impersonating a couple of State men by now?"

"Hard to say; it all depends if the little guy got away. We'll soon find out."

"Not the answer I was looking for, JG."

"Don't worry - trust me."

Now if it was Aquila saying that to me, I wouldn't worry, but Johnny? As we approached the airport, we stopped a fair distance back for we could see the entrance cordoned off by State police, who were stopping everyone and searching them.

"What now, JG?"

"We wait till it's dark and then I create a diversion. When I draw them away, it will give you a chance to slip in."

"What about you?"

"Don't worry about me. I'll meet you at the check-in. I've one or two tricks up my sleeve for them."

"And if you don't make it?"

"If I don't, make sure you're on that plane."

"You sound confident that I'll be able to."

"They'll be looking for two. Give it the superior attitude of an officer that you gave at the pens and you'll be alright."

"But my chip says I'm just a security guy."

"Trust me; by the time you approach those gates, you will be a high-ranking officer. Now we need a place to hide up for a couple of hours."

"But if you can make me an officer, why can't we just walk through the gates together?"

"As I said, they'll be on the look-out for two. Being on your own, you stand a better chance of pulling it off."

"I'm still not happy about leaving you."

"I'll be fine, just pray."

We made our way back to some abandoned buildings and settled down, waiting for the darkness to come. I left Johnny busy with his box of devices, entering codes and data, while I tried to sleep.

His voice woke me.

"Ready, Pastor? It's time to make a move."

As we walked along the highway, we made ourselves scarce when the headlights of State vehicles passed us on the road, heading for the airport.

Standing in the shadows, Johnny said, "That's what we need for you, Pastor, one of those. I'll disappear before the next one comes along. Wave it down, saying that your car was hijacked by the two saboteurs."

"They won't buy that!"

"Listen, with all the chaos going on, and providing you give them that authority voice, they will."

"But you haven't altered my ID yet."

"I did it while you were asleep. If you look at your ensigns, you'll see that they're officer ones. Now go; we don't want to miss that flight."

"What time is it?"

"10 o'clock."

Feeling a bit apprehensive, I watched him disappear into the darkness. "Lord, protect Johnny and help me get away with this," I prayed. I hadn't walked a hundred yards, when I could see the headlights of a car coming. Before I had a chance to flag it down, the car pulled up alongside me and two uniformed men got out, shining their flashlights at me. I knew the best form of defence was attack, so before they had a chance to say anything and with the best authority voice I could muster, I said, "About time too! How long does an officer have to walk these roads before getting a lift?" I walked right past them, opened the rear door and got in.

"Sorry, Sir, we didn't know there was an officer out here," one of them said, closing the door. "Sir, may I ask how you happened to be out here?"

"If you must know, trooper, my car was hijacked by the two saboteurs. I phoned HQ and asked for a car to pick me up. I assumed you were that car."

"No, Sir. We didn't know anything about it; we were patrolling the area on the lookout for them. Where can we take you, Sir?"

With the confidence of knowing that I had nothing to worry about over the ID scanners, I snapped arrogantly, "The airport of course! Where else would I be heading?"

"Yes, Sir; straight away, Sir."

As we approached the long drive to the entrance, I saw a car stop outside the gate and then speed away with a volley of machine gun fire following it. Within a matter of minutes there was chaos, with vehicles from the airport chasing after it and guards running around the perimeter fence, leaving just two guards at the gate. In the confusion, they didn't even look to see who was in the back of the car as we pulled up.

"What's up?" I could hear the driver ask.

"The saboteurs have just tried to get in. They're fools to think that they could just drive in here. No one gets past us," came the reply.

"Apparently they hijacked a State car. They stand no chance of getting away; we'll have them before morning, I know."

"Trooper!" I bellowed from the back, "If you don't move this car I'll have you up on a charge of wasting my time; now move it!"

The car pulled up outside the entrance to the terminal and I sat there waiting for the door of the car to be opened. Not saying a word, I got out and walked towards the automatic doors and into the terminal.

The place was full of State troopers, but thanks to Johnny, I received salute after salute as I made my way to the seating area. To avoid the cameras I kept my head down, looking at my watch. It was 8.30, which left only thirty minutes for Johnny to make it in time to check in, with an hour before the plane was due to leave.

I knew Johnny said that if he didn't make it I had to get on the plane, but the truth was I didn't know if I could leave him there. *Of course he'll make it - he's a resourceful guy. If anyone can do it, it's him. But what if he didn't? He will; I've prayed he will.* The thoughts were going over and over in my head.

"Sir, would you accompany us?" The words made my heart sink. I looked up at two armed men in uniform. "What is it trooper? Why am I being disturbed?"

"If you wouldn't mind coming with us?"

"I'm quite happy here."

"We insist, Sir."

As I didn't want to cause suspicion, I rose to my feet.

"Where are we going?" I demanded petulantly.

"This way, Sir."

With one in front of me and one behind, I knew it was futile trying to escape. We approached two automatic opaque glass doors with guards standing each side. To my surprise they saluted me as we went in.

"Sir, you will be safer here and more comfortable in the officers' lounge. Are you on the London flight?"

"Yes," I replied, amazed and relieved.

"Someone will come for you and escort you to the plane fifteen minutes before boarding. Have a nice flight, Sir."

I took a seat on one of the lounge chairs facing the glass doors so that I could keep an eye out for Johnny.

"I can't wait to get back to the UK; there always seems to be mayhem here."

"Excuse me?" I said, looking up and seeing a tall officer.

"Officer Stanwell, Sir, District 22.

It dawned on me that I hadn't even checked my ID to see if my name was on it, or if it was just letters followed by numbers.

"Sorry. Can you speak up? I'm afraid I've been left a little deaf - with all that gunfire at the gate. What did you say your name was?"

"Officer Stanwell, Sir. Sorry, Sir, I didn't realise you were a high-ranking officer. I hadn't noticed your ensigns. Forgive my intrusion," he said, standing to attention and saluting.

"That's okay, Officer Stanwell; at ease."

I needed to get rid of him, as I didn't want to get tied up in a lengthy conversation, but how? This was an *officer* and, although I was his 'senior', I didn't need any attention brought on by being unfriendly. I could see that he was waiting for me to invite him to sit down, but then a voice from behind him said, "Sir, I'm your escort to the plane."

"Sorry Sir, I have to leave; apparently my plane is waiting."

"Sure, no problem. Have a good flight, Stanwell," I replied with relief.

I was still feeling a bit apprehensive about impersonating an officer and, with only fifteen minutes before my escort arrived, the last thing I wanted was to show any signs of it. I decided that I needed to relax, as all the other officers were doing, so I ordered a coffee. Because my thoughts were on Johnny, I couldn't help looking at my watch and thinking: *where is he?*

"Your coffee, Sir," announced the steward who had brought it to my table.

"Thank you."

Although the coffee was free, I could see that he was hovering - waiting for a tip. I knew I couldn't transfer any credits to him, as it would reveal my identity. I realised this was going to be embarrassing and again it could draw attention to me. Then from behind me, I heard:

"Sorry, Sir. It's time for your flight; we'll have to leave the coffee."

I didn't know how he'd managed it, but standing before me was Johnny. How I maintained my posture as an officer I don't know, but it was a huge relief to see him.

Once the steward had gone, I whispered, "You cut that fine! I'm not going to ask how you managed to be my escort; you can tell me later. What now?"

"We have a flight to board," he replied, walking towards the doors.

The doors opened before us and standing there, about to come in, was the jumped up squirt with two of the biggest guards I'd ever seen – which made him look even smaller.

"Officer Shorts, it's nice to see you again. Your usual table?" asked a steward.

We stood to one side to let him pass, hoping he hadn't recognised us. He strutted past us with his men. As we hastily made our exit through the doors, I whispered to Johnny: "I was hoping Mordecai and Aquila had sorted him out."

"*Stop them!*"

We didn't bother to turn around - it was obvious from his voice that he'd recognised us. We ran down the corridor and out onto the runway with a swarm of troopers after us.

I kept close to Johnny, although where he was going I hadn't a clue. The runway area had a high perimeter fence around it, meaning that the only way out was back the way we came and, with that many men behind us, it would take a miracle for that to happen. But then I had seen several miracles happen these last few days; all I had to do was put my trust in God.

Johnny led me to the fuel depot, where we hid underneath one of the tanker trucks. Fortunately for us it was dark, giving us some protection.

"What do you reckon on our chances, Johnny?"

"In our own strength – useless; but in His, we're home sailing. I'm sure He lets us get into these situations so that He can get us out of them and receive the glory."

"You're right there, Johnny; after all it's all about Him.   Only a few minutes ago I was reminding myself of the miracles we've seen."

"They know we're trapped; they have the main entrance heavily guarded. I think we're safe here for five minutes. Officer Shorts! He sure had the right name given to him. And of all the places that little squirt had to turn up! It's unbelievable! How many lives has he got? I should have thrown him a bit harder when I had the chance," he chuckled.

"Even in a situation like this, Johnny, you can still see the funny side."

"Pastor, the way I see it, you have a choice. I can worry about the situation or laugh. I choose to laugh."

"Well don't laugh too loud; we don't want to draw attention."

"Point taken, Pastor. I have a plan. If this truck has the keys in the ignition, we have a chance of getting out of here. Stay here."

"Pastor, get yourself up here!" came an urgent whisper.

I slid myself from underneath the truck and climbed up into the passenger seat. No sooner was I in, than the truck started up and headed at great speed down the runway.

We soon had a stream of State cars following close behind us. In the distance, above the far end of the runway, I saw a row of bright lights appear. In horror, I realised they were heading towards us, getting lower and lower.

"Johnny, there's a plane coming in towards us!"

It was as if he didn't hear me. We were still in the middle of the runway heading for the plane.

"Johnny! Johnny, the plane!" I cried out as it was almost on top of us.

As I clamped my hand over my eyes, I felt the truck violently swerve to the left out of its path, then came a deafening noise as the landing wheels totalled the cars behind us, that had no chance of getting out of the way in time.

We were heading for the perimeter fence at great speed. I braced myself and waited for the impact, praying that we'd make it through, between the upright steel posts. The sound of the chain link fencing being torn away came to a stop, as the truck embedded itself bonnet-down in a ditch outside the fence.

The next thing I knew was that we were being dragged out of the truck, handcuffed and bundled into the back of a car.

"So you thought you could escape me? Wake up, lowlifes!"

I was still feeling the effects of the impact, and recoiled in pain as his boot crashed into my ribs. I opened my eyes to see the officer that Johnny called 'The Squirt'. Then I noticed Johnny coming around as well and reeling from his boot. We were in a room lying on the floor.

"I just wanted you to see me before I have you taken out and shot."

"Give it your best shot, Squirt," Johnny gasped.

116

Furiously, he barked, "Guards, take them out!"

"Sir, we have orders that the Supreme One wants them alive."

With a look of frustration, he said, "Okay, he can have them alive, but I will *entertain* them tonight."

"Sir, he said alive."

"Oh, I'll make sure they're alive," he said, then added quietly: "*Just.*" He paused for a moment then gave us a venomous glare.

"Well lowlifes, what I have in store for you will be merciful, compared to what the Supreme One has planned for you. Tomorrow you'll be wishing I'd shot you."

The cell door slammed shut, leaving us with our hands cuffed behind our backs. We eased our way so we were sitting with our backs to the wall, facing the cell door.

"Any ideas?" I asked.

"Nope, but I'm sure something will come," he chuckled.

"Ever the optimistic," I replied.

After what seemed like ages, the cell door opened and the two huge guards that had been escorting the officer came in and dragged Johnny out into the cell next door.

I could hear the shrill voice of The Squirt shouting at Johnny. "Who sent you? Who are your contacts? How did you get past security? Where did you get the ID from?" In spite of the situation, I couldn't help smiling to myself as I heard Johnny's reply.

"Father Christmas, you little squirt."

117

"So you think this is funny. Let's see if you laugh at this."

With that, I heard the sound of what I could only imagine was his cane striking Johnny on bare flesh.

"Shall we try that again, lowlife? Who sent you? Who are your contacts?"

"Snow White and the Seven Dwarfs," Johnny laughed.

"So I was not clear enough for you, lowlife? Let's see if you laugh at this."

I cringed at the sound of fists making contact with what I imagined to be Johnny's face. Because everything went quiet, I assumed they had beaten him senseless. *Lord, help him,* I prayed.

"Wake him!" ordered the officer.

I could only just hear the sound of Johnny's voice as he groaned, "Do that again, and it will be the last thing you do."

"What did he say?" said Officer Shorts to the guard that was leaning over Johnny.

He said, "Do it again, Sir".

"Strike him!" he bellowed, "I *will* have the information out of him, for the Supreme One tomorrow!"

I steeled myself to hear a repeat of the sound of Johnny taking a battering, but it didn't materialise. What I did hear was screaming and what sounded like bodies being thrown hard against the dividing wall. I didn't know what had taken place next door, but it didn't sound like Johnny screaming.

As I sat there waiting, I heard my cell door being unlocked. I knew I shouldn't fear, but I just didn't know if it was now my turn to experience the same fate as Johnny. I closed my eyes and prayed.

"You going to sit there all night, or are we going to get out of this place?"

I opened my eyes and saw Johnny standing there.   "What... how...?"

"I'll tell you on the way, Pastor, but first I need to get the stuff the little squirt took from me. Now, let's get these cuffs off you."

"Do you know where it is?"

"I assume his office, wherever that is."

I could see he was glowing with confidence as we walked down the corridor to a closed steel door.

"You look as if you've got war paint on your face with those red stripes on your cheeks."

"Don't get me going, Pastor."

"Locked. Now what?" I asked him.

"We knock."

"We knock! I should have thought that's the last thing we want to do."

"Well, how else do you suppose we're going to get it opened?"

Johnny knocked loudly. The sliding steel hatch on the door opened and a guard's face appeared.

"We're done here," Johnny announced.

"Yes, Sir."

We stood back as the door opened towards us.

"Keep this door locked - no matter what you hear. Those men are lowlifes! The small one is particularly troublesome - trying to pretend he's an officer. Don't be fooled. Do you understand? I'll be back in the morning."

"Yes, Sir."

As we walked towards what we assumed was the office, I asked: "What happened back there? How come he didn't question who you were?"

"Pastor, I thought by now you'd realise that we're operating in the supernatural realm."

"This level of supernatural is a little new to me; I keep forgetting."

"Faith and boldness, Pastor. It will get you anywhere."

"You're preaching faith to me?"

"Ha, there it is; that little squirt was so keen to get at us he hasn't even looked in my bag. Right, Pastor, let's get out of here."

"Is that with faith or boldness?"

"Now you're getting it, Pastor."

And so with faith and boldness we walked past all the guards and out into the compound towards the main gates.

"Stop. We're going back," he said turning around.

"What! Going back? Are you insane?"

I had no choice but to follow him, so as not to draw attention to us. Johnny approached one of the guards standing outside the building and said, "Have the officers' car brought round."

"Yes, Sir."

Within a minute an official car drove up.

"We don't need a driver – that's my job," he said to the trooper.

The driver got out, and saluted as he opened the rear door for me.

As we headed out into the darkness of the quiet roads, I said, "So how did you get out of that cell?"

"It was beautiful. There was that little squirt trying to break his cane on my face, and his two henchmen using me as their punch bag, when I must have passed out.

The next thing I knew, I was saying, "Do that again and it will be the last thing you do." Suddenly the room filled with a mighty flash and Mordecai was standing there.

Those two didn't know what hit them. And the little squirt - I almost felt sorry for him. You should have seen his face as Mordecai approached him. There he was frantically trying to unlock the door, then he just crumpled to the floor, fainting from fear. You've heard the expression: 'white as a sheet'? Well, that would describe his face all right. Then, as I stepped over him to go out the door, he must have moved and come into contact with my boot, because he let out a little groan."

"Did you apologise?"

"Of course," he said laughing, "but he shouldn't have moved."

"So where now?"

"We head south."

"Why south?"

"It's the least obvious. The options are: north of Tel Aviv are Netanya and Haifa, but they'll be too heavily guarded. To the east is the broader crossing to Jordan: that too will be heavily guarded. We could try crossing the river, but I think it's a no-no. Going south would give us choices. There's a small airfield after Tzomet Shizafona - we may be able to get a plane, but somehow I think we wouldn't get far. Or we get a ship from Ashdod or Eilat, which is the furthest point south. And of course there's Eilat Airport - we could fly to Jordan."

"So how far is that?"

"About 354 kilometres - four hour drive (before you say it). I know it's a long way, but the terrain is less populated and it's less risky than going north.

I reckon we've got about a couple of hours of darkness left; we need to go as far as we can before daybreak in this car, then ditch it, and the uniforms, before the little squirt gets let out of that cell. He's supposed to take us to 'The Supreme One' and he knows he's in trouble, so he'll try to hunt us down with all he's got. You'd think he would have given up, having experienced Mordecai the first time."

"Yeah, you would think so. But then, he knows it's his neck on the chopping block or ours. I think he won't give up until he finds us."

10

"**P**astor, wake up. Time to get going."

"What time is it?"

"Dawn, and there's a cracker of a sunrise."

Stepping out of the car, I could see what Johnny meant. The view from our position near the top of the mountain was spectacular. As far as the eye could see was a panorama of misty, blue mountains, outlined in a fiery red from the sun as it lit up the morning sky.

"Johnny, whereabouts are we?"

"I think we're on Mitzpeh Sayarim, by the view; I'm not too familiar with the land this far south."

"So over there, where the sun is coming up, is Hazeva?"

"I'm impressed, Pastor."

"Johnny, I think you should come and see this."

"I've already seen it."

"No, not the sunrise, *that.*"

"What! I don't believe that little squirt! How did he track us this far?"

Heading our way, on the road below, was a convoy of car headlights. "How's that possible, Johnny? I thought we were the ones with the technology."

"Of course - the car! I didn't demobilise its tracker. We shouldn't have stopped."

"How long before he's here?"

"I reckon, if we leave now, we'll have a 30 minutes' head start; but first I'm going to do what I should have done when we got in the car: turn off the tracker. I must be slipping, Pastor."

"What about these uniforms?"

"Well, I don't know about you, Pastor, but it's too chilly to be hiking in my underwear," he said chuckling. "No, we'll find some replacements on our travels. Now, unless you want to wait here for them, I suggest we make tracks now. It's about 20 kilometres to Eilat (about 12 miles to you) and that's by foot.

We made our way down; the road went to the right and ahead of us was the desert.

"What you reckon, Pastor, the road or the desert?"

"If we take the road, they'll be on us in no time."

"True. It's up to you."

"Why me?"

"Because if it goes wrong, I don't want it to come back on me. Anyway, it's your chance to show leadership - after all, you are a pastor."

I knew that wasn't the reason he didn't want to choose. "If we take the desert, won't we get lost?"

"Most probably; that's if we don't die of thirst, having no water with us."

"Lord, which way?" I prayed. The words: '*The desert*', were gently whispered in my ear.

"We take the desert!"

"You heard from the Lord, didn't you? *That's* what I wanted, Pastor. You see, in the natural realm, both ways would lead to death. At least this way, if the squirt wants to follow us, it means he will have to ditch the cars. Unless he's towing a camel behind him, we have an even chance of keeping ahead of him."

"How would he know what direction we took from the mountain?"

"It's pretty obvious; he knows Eilat is the only place to escape this far south. Somehow, we need to get out of these uniforms before we get there, so we can blend in with the locals. Pray for some assistance, Pastor."

Knowing that the Lord answers my prayers, I prayed: "Lord, I know we're in the middle of nowhere and we're being pursued, but we need a change of clothes." I knew that, in the natural realm, it was virtually impossible, but then I knew that with Him all things are possible.

"As we remember what you did for the Israelites when they were trapped between the Egyptian army and the Red Sea, I'm asking Lord for your help; for you, Lord, are the same today as you were yesterday."

"Pastor, cover your face - there's a sand storm ahead of us."

"Where did that come from? I didn't pray for that; it's all we need. "

"That's *exactly* what we need; we can lose ourselves in it, if he was stupid enough to follow us. Keep close, Pastor, I'm not losing you out here."

Even though I kept my head down, the sand stung the exposed skin on my hands and cheeks. I could just make out the shape of Johnny alongside me as we slowly made our way ahead.

We had spent what seemed liked hours battering our way through the storm, when I realised Johnny was shouting at me.

"Pastor, look – Bedouins!"

"What?" I shouted, hardly able to hear him.

"*Bedouins* – Nomads. We'll take shelter there!" he shouted.

Raising my head a little, I could see that, in the middle of nowhere, was a cluster of tents.

"Stay here, Pastor; I won't be long."

Johnny made his way over and disappeared into one of the tents. Within a few minutes he came out and beckoned me to follow. We went inside, which was a most welcome break, away from the stinging sand storm.

I couldn't believe how cosy and warm it was inside. Sitting on the floor were what I assumed were the head tribesmen. I followed Johnny's lead and sat down facing them. Plates of food and drink were placed in front of us.

"Don't ask what it is; just eat," Johnny whispered in my ear. "We don't want to offend them. By the way use your right hand only to eat."

The Headman lent over to the man on his right and spoke to him; in turn the man spoke to Johnny in a language I'd never heard before. To my amazement, Johnny answered in the strange language.

"What did he say?" I asked.

"He said that his master says that his home is ours and that it is an honour to have such important guests and we're welcome to stay until the storm passes."

126

I couldn't help noticing that the eyes of all the people in the tent watched every mouthful of food I swallowed. I soon realised that they were looking for approval. Even though some mouthfuls contained something gristly, my 'audience' made it impossible for me to spit it out, leaving me no option but to swallow it.

To give them the result they were looking for, I mustered a false smile, but even taking a mouthful of coffee didn't help - it was so gritty, I was sure that it had sand in it. I found out later from Johnny that the grittiness was the norm for their coffee. I was sure I heard a quiet little chuckle from him. *He's loving this*, I thought to myself.

The Headman spoke again, which was a relief for me, as all eyes went to him. The conversation between his man and Johnny went on for some time. I sat there patiently waiting for them to finish, and then finally I asked, "What was that all about?"

"He wanted to know why two important people were this far south and away from the rest of the convoy, but he sensed that we were in trouble.

I explained that we were not important people but were being pursued by the State police. I told him that we had to get to Eilat to escape them, but we needed to change our clothes.

He said that the State police were not welcome and that they have had confrontations with them in the past. Even though they are their enemies, they are bound by their custom to feed and protect them if they came into this camp as we have.

I asked him why he thought we were important people. Apparently they had been watching us last night and they knew God was with us, because standing outside the car were two mighty warriors guarding it, a man and a woman."

"Mordecai and Aquila?" I asked.

"Sounds like it, Pastor. That accounts for the fact that, when I walked into their tent, there wasn't any trouble. To these people that would be a mighty sign and they are people who believe in God; also they are of the land and there's nothing they don't seem to know. I shouldn't tell you this, but he says the Sheik says you have a trustworthy face."

"Sheik?"

"Headman."

"Thank him for his hospitality and tell him that God will bless him and his people. He speaks the truth."

"About what?"

"My trustworthy face."

"Yeah sure, Pastor."

The tent curtain was drawn to one side and one of the tribesmen came in. In an agitated voice he spoke to the Sheik; his man then turned to Johnny and spoke to him.

"What's up?" I asked.

"Apparently the little squirt and his men have gone into Eilat."

"Is that good, or bad for us?"

"Well both. Good because, as he said, that means we'll be under their protection; but bad because the squirt will have his men guard the port and airfield. I was hoping to have got on the ship or plane before they got there, but at least now we'll have time to plan. Sounds like the storm has passed."

Johnny spoke to the Sheik's man.

"What did you say to him?"

128

"I asked if we could stay the night."

"And?"

"He said his master said we're welcome, but you with the trustworthy face must sleep with his master's camels, to keep them company."

"Very funny."

We were shown to a tent where we were to rest.

"These Bedouin people: do they live out here all the time?"

"Ready for a little Bedouin history lesson?

"Sounds as if I'm going to get one again, ready or not," I sighed.

"What do you mean: 'again'?"

"The last one was all about the tunnel and stones, remember?"

"Well, I reckon, while you're out here, it's to your advantage to know all there is to know. Do I hear a 'thank you'?"

"Get on with it."

"The majority of Bedouins in Israel (approximately 160,000) live in the Negev, with another 70,000 in Galilee. About half of Israeli Bedouins originated in tribes that emerged from Arabian deserts in the seventh century. They eventually migrated north to the Negev by way of Iraq and Syria. The other half are divided into groups: farmers from Egypt and Sinai (who came north during later Turkish times) and tribes people from Sudan (who arrived in the 19th century as slaves).

The Bedouins' livelihoods once depended entirely on moving their flocks through the desert from well to well and from pasture to pasture. Now, most have settled down permanently. However, among the elements of the Bedouin culture still powerfully evident are (as we have experienced): hospitality and ties of family, tribes and confederation.

"Wow, how do you know all this stuff? I'm impressed."

"Oh, it comes naturally to me; I told you I'm good."

"Yeah, yeah, so you say. So how?"

"Internet."

"I knew you weren't *that* good. So that's what you were doing while talking to me. I could see you glancing down at your pad."

"Well I answered your question didn't I?"

"I suppose you had a translator on your pad when the Headman was talking?"

"No, I speak seven languages, including theirs."

"I'm not going to ask what they are - your head's big enough as it is."

"Some of us have bigger heads than others, Pastor."

"So, if what you say is true about the Bedouins being located mostly in the north, the chance of them being this far south is rather remote; and the fact they were right where we needed help, I would say that's more than a coincidence, wouldn't you?"

"I would call it an answer to prayer. When we came off that mountain we could have turned right to avoid the desert. After all, to go into the desert without any water would be considered suicidal; but He planned for that Bedouin tribe to be in the right place at the right time."

"It's good to know He's there for us. On another subject, what was I eating back there?"

"What did it taste like?"

"That's the thing - I don't know; it was a little spicy but very gristly. I had to force myself to swallow it."

"That was the good part."

"Good part? I know we're supposed to be thankful for our food, but I don't know if you can call that food. It had the most foul taste I've ever tasted. So what was it?"

"Well now, it could have been snake or maybe camel, but most probably goats' intestines or eyes."

"Are you serious? Tell me you're joking."

"Let's put it this way, they eat what they can get their hands on out here and that includes every bit of the animal."

"Remind me not to have breakfast. Now, can we change the subject?"

"It was *your* subject. Where are you going?"

"Call of nature."

As I made my way out of the tent I was taken aback by the night sky. I had looked up into the night sky many times but never seen it like I was seeing it now; it was as if I could touch each star, the sky was so clear. I realised the scene must have been like the one Abraham saw when God told him to look up into the night sky. Mesmerised by it all, I had a job to draw myself away, but eventually the cold of the night made me re-enter the tent.

"You were a long time. Did you get lost or something?"

"No, I was admiring God's creation."

"Beautiful isn't it? You never see the sky anywhere else like it is out here, with nothing to pollute it. I've got many stories of sleeping out in the desert under the stars. Yes, it's something to be in awe of."

131

I was awoken by the voices of Johnny and another man in the tent.

"What's up?" I asked.

"The Sheik wants to see us. We'd better get a move on; it's not good to keep him waiting."

We entered his tent and sat before him. Immediately one of the women brought in food and drink. As the food looked like some form of bread, I received it and ate it while listening to the Sheik's man and Johnny exchanging words. He rose from his cushion, so we did the same, and followed him outside.

"Ever ridden a camel before, Pastor? If you haven't, you're going to get a chance now. We're going into Eilat with him and a few of his men, and we'll be disguised as Bedouins."

"What about these uniforms?"

"I think the answer to that problem is behind you, Pastor."

I turned and standing there was a woman with several articles of clothing, beckoning us to go into a tent.

"You first, Pastor. I'm going to enjoy this."

I stood there while the woman decked me in various layers of clothing. As she added each layer, I gestured with my hands to ask what it was called. "Sirwal" she answered as she wrapped the first piece around my body. The next item I found out was called a 'tob', or what I would call a full-length robe, and then over this she put a 'redan', a striped sleeveless coat. (Apparently the Sheik said that we had to be dressed in that to show status - because we were important people.)

Next was the 'kufeya', the headpiece; I recognised that from many films I'd seen, although I hadn't known what it was called.

It was the final part I was taken aback by. She applied a thick paste-like substance over my face, hands and feet that made my skin tanned like the skin of the tribe. I didn't ask what it was – I preferred not to know.

"If I didn't know you, Pastor, I would take you for a Bedouin. And you smell like one too - or at least one of their camels," he chuckled.

"You'll keep till we get back home, Johnny," I assured him as I put on the sandals she gave me.

When she had finished with Johnny, we were taken over towards the camels.

"How do I get up there?"

Before Johnny answered, one of the men said something to the camel and it went down on its knees. I watched Johnny get on and followed his actions.

"Hold on firmly to the pommel of the saddle," he called out.

I soon found out why, as the camel quickly stood up and I was tipped onto the sand.

"Obviously not firm enough. I told you to hang on," he said with a smug grin.

Once again the camel lowered itself and this time I was ready. So, being led by the Sheik, we set off on the most uncomfortable journey I've ever taken. The only consolation was that it was not that many kilometres.

Eventually we came out of the desert and onto a road. Ahead, at the entrance to Eilat, was a blockade of trucks and police, stopping everyone who was trying to enter.

When it was our turn, to my surprise, the guard waved us through. We asked no questions and just followed the Sheik.

It wasn't long before we came to a stop outside a large, beautifully decorated building. The tall, automatic black and gold gates opened. Inside was a courtyard paved with white marble, in the centre of which was a huge fountain. A team of men quickly made their way over to the Sheik as his camel lowered itself to the ground. There was a lot of hand-clapping and raised voices from the men who greeted us as more servants came hurrying over.

Johnny spoke to the man who rode alongside him.

"What did you say?"

"I asked whose place this was? He said it was his master's. He is obviously someone of importance and very wealthy."

"Obviously; but what's he doing, living in the desert in a tent?"

"I dare say we'll find out. Meanwhile, it looks as if we're to follow his man."

We followed him into the house and were shown into a room of sheer luxury. Before he left he spoke to Johnny.

"We're to freshen up and dine with the Sheik tonight, to hear his plan for our escape. Meanwhile we're free to go wherever we like in the grounds."

"I wonder if this place has a bath. I don't know about you, but I could sure do with one. That stuff on my skin has baked on with the hot sun."

After exploring several rooms, I found a bathroom fit for a king. I had never bathed in such luxury. It was more of a marble pool than a bath, with gold taps and statues that the water cascaded from. *Who is this man?* I mused, as I wallowed in the water.

My me-time was interrupted by Johnny shouting from behind the door, "Are you still alive? You've been in there over an hour. There's a change of clothes for you in the other room."

"You don't know what you're missing. This is sheer bliss; you should try it."

"I already have. I've got my own bathroom; in fact there're three in this section of the house. You'd better get yourself ready, so we don't keep him waiting when we're called."

On my bed was laid out an eastern-style pure silk outfit, which I assumed was for dining in. Having put it on, I made my way into the main room of our suite where Johnny was lounging in a chair.

"You look the part, Pastor."

"So do you, Johnny."

As we spoke there was a knock at the door, then a man entered who spoke in English.

"My master has requested your company; please follow."

We followed him into a large room where the Sheik was seated at a long table and several servants were standing round the room.

"Come, sit," he said in English.

"You speak English?" I said, surprised.

"Yes, Pastor. I spent five years at Cambridge University. My family insisted that I learned English and western ways. Now, first we eat then we discuss how we're to arrange your escape."

Within moments, the table was filled with a variety of foods served on silver platters.

"Don't worry, Pastor, there are no sheep eyes or camel tongues."

Johnny gave out a loud laugh.

When we had finished dining, we followed him outside where we sat by (what I guess was) an Olympic-sized swimming pool.

"Now, Johnny Gold, or should I call you 'Yitzhak Goldstein' of Shaldag, an elite Israeli Air Force commando unit, considered the best in the world? And you received the highest award for bravery: the Medal of Valour? Yes, Johnny Gold 777, I know all there is to know about you. Pastor, we have in our company a war hero."

"Please don't call me that. I'm no war hero; I'm just an ordinary guy who did what he had to do for a friend. How did you know my name - especially my real name? Nobody knows that, except the Pastor here, and he's only just found out. And my activities with Shaldag? That's highly classified."

"I have 'ears' all over the world, Johnny Gold; there's nothing that I cannot find out about. You see, my intelligence service makes the World Government's secrecy futile. Now, what I know of you, Pastor, is somewhat sketchy. My people tell me that the information on you only goes back a little while, but I've instructed them to find out. It is not an option for me to be ignorant of what goes on.

I also know it was the two of you who were responsible for the chaos in Jerusalem. I can see that the words of your God, which are being transmitted, are powerful - by the reaction of the authorities, who are trying desperately to shut it down.

Now to my plan: Tomorrow we will go to the airport. My pilot is waiting to fly you to Jordan, where I have a private airfield. I will have a change of clothes brought to you in the morning. Your uniforms will be on the plane so that you can change back into them if you should need to. I'm sorry, Pastor, but you will have to put up with the coating on your skin again. Your white skin would give my plan away."

"What should we call you? Is it: 'Your Royal Highness' or 'Prince Hashem bin Al Hussein', from the House of Hashemites?

"I compliment you, Johnny Gold, on your homework. Just 'Hash' will do."

"You see, you're not the only one who knows things."

"May I ask you when you knew who I was?"

"When we came into the property. I noticed the plaque on the wall with the Royal Seal outside the entrance. Then I observed a painting on the wall in the hall of you with your family. I knew straight away who you were, Prince Hashem. I've got one question, or the Pastor does."

"Ask."

"Why does a prince, a man of great wealth, choose to live in a tent in the desert?"

A smile came across his face.

"For two weeks of the year I escape to the desert to remind me of my roots. It is good for a person to be as one with the desert; it is good for the soul and spirit."

"I can understand that. Jesus often went away to a place of solitude," I said.

"I know of your Jesus, Pastor, - a prophet. But my religion has its own prophet. I would love to discuss our beliefs but we need to rest. We leave early in the morning."

11

We were woken by a man coming into our quarters. In English he said, "You must rise; it is time."

When he had finished dressing us in our outfits, I couldn't resist looking in the ornate gold mirror; even I had to admit we looked convincing. We were to be part of the royal entourage going to Eilat. Dark glasses were the final touch.

He escorted us outside, where I was half-expecting to have to climb onto a camel again; I was relieved to see several limousines. Our man led us to the front limousine, with its darkened windows and a royal flag on the bonnet.

"Good morning. Are we ready, gentlemen? You have a plane to catch. If, by chance, you are spoken to at the airport, don't say anything; I have people that speak for me. It shouldn't happen as they know who I am and I have never been stopped. We'll go straight to my plane, which will be waiting. Walk with confidence and superiority; stay close to me, and you will be fine."

"Sounds good to us," Johnny replied.

"By the way, for infidels, you scrub up well," Hash laughed.

"Lord, you sure have a sense of humour, surrounding me with people who like a joke," I said under by breath.

A cheerful heart is good medicine, instantly entered my head.

With an air of importance, we entered Eilat, passing through a checkpoint where the guards waved us on. It wasn't long before we approached the entrance of the airport, where several cars were waiting in a queue. Each car was stopped and searched before they were let through.

When it was our turn, we were flagged down. The driver's window lowered.

"Would you all please step out of the car," said a guard who looked very young.

"Drive on!" ordered Hash's right-hand man, who was sitting in the front passenger seat.

The driver's window started to rise and the car moved off.

"Stop!" demanded the young guard, who was now joined by other armed guards and they quickly surrounded the car.

Hash showed no concern about what was going on outside. Very calmly his man stepped out of the car and approached the guards. He bellowed:

"Do you *know* who you are *inconveniencing* you infidel?"

"No," the young guard replied nervously.

"You are holding up my master, His Royal Highness, Prince Hashem bin Al Hussein, from the House of Hashemites. Now stand aside and let us through!"

"But, Sir, I have my orders – not to let anyone through without searching the cars."

"Then, Son of a Camel, you will have to shoot us because we're going through."

The young guard looked at the others, who looked back helplessly, not knowing what to do. Hash's man got back in the car and instructed the driver to drive on. The guards had no choice but to step out of the way. As the car passed the young guard I could see he was making a frantic phone call. I could only guess that it was to his superior who was somewhere in the airport building.

As our car passed the main entrance of the building, Johnny announced, "Well, well, if it's not my little friend, Officer Squirt." He had just come out of the building. Our car sped on past him on its way to the runway, and he was soon in hot pursuit with his men.

The car came to a halt, metres away from the plane; Hash's man jumped out of the car and instructed the two cars that were following us to form a barricade between the plane and the armed guards, who had clambered out of their cars at great speed.

"You will *not* board the plane!" commanded the officer.

Hash's men drew their weapons ready to defy him.

As the officer and his guards could see that being out in the open would make them easy pickings in an exchange of gunfire, they retreated behind their cars. The officer gave his orders again, "Lay down your weapons and step away from the plane!"

141

"Do you think he knows it is *us* trying to get on that plane?" I asked Johnny.

"I'm not sure, but I think he's not taking any chances. He knows that we'll be heading for Eliat, as our only means of escape, and possibly already knows somehow that we're here. As Hash's people are the only ones that have not been stopped, he obviously wants to make sure we're not amongst them."

"If you don't lay down your weapons we'll open fire," came a second warning.

Hash's men remained steadfast with not a waver of nerves amongst them.

"Fire!" shouted the little officer.

A volley of fire hit our cars, with an exchange of fire from Hash's men.

"Gentlemen, go now with my pilot. I will clear up this little misunderstanding."

"Will you be okay, Hash?" I said, concerned.

"Sure. They will not want a diplomatic situation. Now go and may your God go with you, my friends," he said as he kissed us on both cheeks.

We followed the pilot up the steps to the plane, but a bullet stopped him before he got to the top. Johnny caught him before he tumbled back down the steps.

"He's been shot, Johnny!"

My words made Hash turn around.

"He's okay, Hash. The bullet caught his arm, but he's in no shape to fly," said Johnny.

"Now what?" I said, alarmed.

"You take the plane, Johnny Gold. I will have it picked up."

"Don't tell me you can fly that?"

"Pastor, if it has wings, I can fly it."

"We'll keep their heads down. Now go!" said Hash.

The continuous fire from Hash's men gave us time to get on board. In no time the plane was moving down the runway at great speed.

"There's a truck coming at us from the other end, Johnny!" I yelled.

"I can see that, Pastor; trust me I know what I'm doing."

"It's a bit late for that."

"I got you out of the last runway episode with the plane, didn't I? And this is only a truck."

"Yes, but we ended up in a ditch and being caught."

"A minor detail, Pastor. We escaped, didn't we?"

With that Johnny applied full throttle. As the jets roared, the wheels of the plane barely cleared the roof of the truck.

"That was close!"

"No, that was precision flying, Pastor. I told you that you could trust me."

It wasn't long before we were up amongst the clouds.

"It feels safe up here - closer to God," I said as I sat back and relaxed after such a heart-racing experience.

"I know what you mean. I always felt that in my flying days."

"So where are we heading for?"

"I think Hash intended us to go to Jordan, but what about heading for home?"

"Home would be great. How far is that?"

"2,250 nautical miles, there about."

"In this?"

"Pastor, this baby has a full tank and a range of 3,000 miles. Oh yes, this will fly us home. So, is it Jordan or home?"

"Let's go home, Johnny. I have a promise to keep."

"I was hoping you'd say that."

12

"**S**orry to wake you, Pastor, but we've got company."

"We've what?" I said, blearily.

"Look out of your window to the left: a State fighter coming in fast."

"Is he intending to shoot us down?"

"If he was, he could have done that already. No, he's been sent to make us turn around; Squirt wants us back alive so he can hand us over to his boss."

"Can't we out-fly him?"

"Even if we could, we couldn't out-fly his missiles. Unless we have a miracle, Pastor, we have no hope."

"Well then, we ask for one, Johnny."

I could see the fighter pilot, who was now alongside us. Instructions to turn around came over the radio from him. Johnny turned it off. Seeing no response, the pilot gestured with his hand for us to turn around.

"He's telling us to turn around, Johnny."

"I can see him."

"So, are we going to?

I felt the plane bank down as we veered to the left. The fighter plane did the same and was heading back, obviously thinking we were going to follow. All of a sudden our plane went vertical, turning us upside down, and headed in the opposite direction.

"What are you doing"?

"I decided for the miracle, Pastor."

"Why isn't he giving chase?"

"He hasn't got to; in fact he won't want to be too close when his missile hits. Brace yourself, Pastor, it's going to get a little wild."

"I thought you said the Squirt wanted us back?"

"He'd rather shoot us down than let us escape; that would be inexcusable to his boss."

As Johnny finished speaking, he put the plane into a violent spin and a missile missed us by a whisker.

"That was close!" I said as the plane levelled.

"It's not over yet. Look ahead."

The missile had turned around and was coming straight for us. I could see by Johnny's calm face that his fighter pilot training was automatically kicking in, yet this was no fighter jet but a private plane with no weapons and not enough speed to outmanoeuvre a missile. I knew it was just matter of time before it was all over. I wasn't a hundred percent sure but I thought I detected a little smile on Johnny's face. *He's enjoying this!* I thought.

"Johnny! Why are you taking us towards the other plane?"

He didn't answer. I could see out of the window that the missile was just metres away, and in front was the fighter jet coming at us.

146

"*Johnny!*" I screeched, when our plane veered violently upward, but not before our tail was caught in the blast of the explosion between the fighter plane and the missile. Instantly we went into a dive, and as we came through the clouds I could see the sea coming up towards us rapidly.

"Blast it! We've lost the tail, Pastor. I must be getting old or something; it appears I'm not as good as I used to be. If you're thinking of praying for that miracle, now would be a good time, as we have seconds before we hit the sea."

I shut my eyes ready for the impact, knowing I didn't have time for any prayer, but only the word: 'Jesus'. Then, instead of the impact, I felt the plane level out.

"Pastor, you'd better open your eyes and see this. Our miracle has turned up, or I should say *miracles.*"

I opened my eyes and there, holding each wing up, were Mordecai and Aquila.

"We're flying on angel power, Pastor. Unbelievable, isn't it?"

I smiled and found myself saying, "Not with God, Johnny. However, I feel sorry for the fighter pilot."

"He reaped what he sowed. His own missile hit him, and unfortunately the blast damaged our tail. The last I saw, bits of his plane were hitting the sea."

"You were enjoying yourself back there, playing cat and mouse with that missile weren't you?"

"Why do you say that?"

"I couldn't help noticing a little smile on your face."

"Really? I can assure you, Pastor, inside I was as scared as you."

"But I thought, having been in the armed forces, you were trained for that stuff?"

"That was a long time ago, and I'll tell you a little secret: it's fear that kept me alive (and, of course, training in how to out-manoeuvre a missile)."

"Is that what you were doing back there?"

"Trying to, but it helps if you're in a plane that's got the right equipment. My fighter jet was equipped with a countermeasure called a 'jammer', as well as a simpler form of countermeasure called 'chaff' (small strips of metal that reflect radar beams and confuse the missile's onboard radar).

There are a lot more techniques and skills a pilot can use but I don't want to be accused of being too technical for you."

"Thank the dear Lord for that. Seriously though, Johnny, I might not understand the technical stuff, but in a simple way it all makes sense to me. There's a sermon that I preached once that's just come back to me. It was about a person who steps out of the Lord's protection and opens himself up to the fiery darts of the devil. They're like heat-seeking missiles and the only hope of them not striking and destroying, is the counter measure of the Lord, which is to run back into his presence."

"That's pretty good, Pastor, do you want me to carry on?"

"There's more?"

"A bit more but I can leave it there if it's too much?"

"No, honestly I do find it interesting; carry on."

"The launch of a heat-seeking missile can be detected by MWS (missile warning sensors), which are small cameras placed all around the aircraft.

These cameras detect missile smoke plumes and warn the pilot with the direction of the smoke plume. The pilot can respond by launching flares to spoof the missile's infrared camera, and/or reducing his own heat signature by powering back his engines.

There's a strategy called 'Missile end-game defence': If the missile cannot be defeated kinematically (which is even more technical to go into), it will continue towards the pilot until impact is imminent.

At this point the pilot must begin an end-game defence. Typically these are high-speed, high-g slices (descending turns) that give the aircraft the highest line-of-sight rate across the missile's field of view. This forces the missile to make a very hard, high-g turn in order to stay with the pilot. The more energy the pilot is able to force the missile to bleed off before the end-game, the less energy the missile will have available to make this turn. Ideally the missile will either a) not have enough energy to complete the turn, and fall short of the aircraft (and then self-destruct), or b) will be travelling so fast that it cannot make a sharp enough turn to stay with the pilot in the slice, and will overshoot (and then self-destruct)."

"Is that what happened back there between the missile and the fighter jet?"

"Yes, but it didn't self-destruct; it found a heat source: the jet. Where was I? Oh yes, during this point, copious amounts of chaff (or flare) are also dispensed. There's a whole lot more to it but let's just say there are a wealth of strategic measures available to a trained pilot with a properly equipped plane.

So I can assure you, Pastor, the fact that I was in an ordinary jet without any form of defence, meant I was scared. What am I saying? I was petrified. I'm not superhuman, Pastor."

"I must confess, Johnny, I was beginning to think you were, with all your skills and knowledge."

"No, Pastor, just a normal guy like you.'"

"A normal guy doesn't know all that stuff; a normal guy isn't a hero; a normal guy doesn't speak every language under the sun; a normal guy doesn't do all the things you can do."

"You're wrong there, Pastor, I only speak seven languages."

"Seven isn't *normal*. So, tell me, Johnny, how did you get that Medal of Valour?"

"It's something I don't really like talking about; it brings up too many memories."

"I thought that was the case when Hash called you a war hero. He probably thought you would have been proud of such an act of bravery."

"For my friend - yes, for me - no."

"It sounds as if, whatever it was, it's deep within you still. Being a pastor, Johnny, I've done a lot of counselling, and talking about it can bring release. Why don't you try telling me and if it gets too much just stop?"

"Stop me if I get into too much detail; I know I've a tendency to do that, but it was my training - having to fill out so many detailed reports after a mission."

"I've noticed that you're a person of details, Johnny. Please - carry on."

"I had a friend, David. As boys, we did everything together and, when we were of age, we were called up. We had decided as lads that, when the time came, we would join the airforce, even though it meant a conscription of nine years, as opposed to three for the army. We'd always fancied flying rather than being on the ground.

We'd made a pact that, flying on a mission together, we would always have each other's backs. Our job was aerial reconnaissance and we would take turns: one would fly and the other would take photos.

One morning we were sent out on separate missions. When I got back I was informed that David had been shot down, some 150 kilometres from the border, but that he had managed to bail out.

I asked my superior if I could go and get him. He replied that he knew how close we were and said that, if I did, I would be on my own as they couldn't spare any men and that my chances of making it in and out were very slim. Even so, I had no choice. He was out there, at the mercy of an enemy that hated us Jews, and I knew that he would have come for me.

I kept thinking of the plans we had discussed, about starting a private flying school when we were discharged in four weeks' time from service.

My commander arranged to have a helicopter at my disposal. Although slower and less armed than my jet, it meant I could fly low over the terrain and land close by. I knew I had twenty-four hours before the battery on his homing device died.

I flew under cover of darkness towards the location. I didn't even know if he was alive, and his homing signal was failing, but I had to try, even if it meant bringing back his body for his family.

I was within 5 kilometres of the signal and decided it was safer to make the rest of the journey on foot, so as not to give away his location. I was

151

fortunate to land in a small clearing in a wood, and, making sure the coast was clear, I continued towards the signal using my hand-held homer.

The further into the woods I went, the denser it got. The thought of him and his parachute landing amongst the trees increased the likelihood of him not being alive.

The homing device told me he was somewhere near. With my eyes scanning the treetops, I saw him, dangling some 5-metres up from a tree branch. "David!" I called out quietly. There was no response; his body hung limply from the tangled parachute caught in the tree.

I climbed the tree to get alongside him and eased my way along the branch so I could tie a rope around him. To my relief, I could see he was still breathing but badly wounded. I made the rope secure by lashing it to another branch and started to cut him free from his harness. He dropped down a short way taking up the slack in the rope. I held the rope with one hand and untied it. Slowly I lowered him to the ground.

Climbing down I could see the extent of his injuries; he had been hit by shrapnel to the chest and side as his plane was shot down. From my backpack I applied, the best I could, a bandage; but because he had lost a lot of blood I could see he was in no fit state to travel. I knew that If I tried to move him the shrapnel could kill him.

"David, it's me," I said, as I put water to his mouth. He gave a cough and opened his eyes.

"Yitzhak, my friend. I knew you would find me," he whispered as he squeezed my hand. And with that he passed out again.

I knew his injuries needed urgent medical attention, but that was easier said than done; we were 150 kilometres behind enemy lines. Fortunately my helicopter was only 5k away, but with someone who couldn't possibly walk it might as well have been 150.

There was only one thing for it; I would have to make a stretcher and drag him the 5k. I cut some branches and lashed them together with the cords of the parachute and attached its harness to it, which enabled me to drag him behind me.

The going was tough, winding in and out of the trees and having to stop frequently to free off the stretcher frame when it got snagged in the undergrowth. Every ounce of my strength and endurance was being put to the test, but all I knew was I couldn't give up. *Just one more step,* I kept telling myself. Repeating those words paid off; I could see, by the moonlight, the clearing in the woods and the helicopter.

My training told me to assess the situation. Not knowing who was out there, I waited. I needed a clear mind and, more importantly, strength, to move quickly the last 25 metres. In sheer exhaustion, I collapsed to the ground behind a fallen tree. I don't know how long I had been lying there, but I was woken by voices.

I quickly unhitched myself from the harness. The voices were coming from the helicopter. There were two armed men by it. Understanding their language, I realised they were talking about searching the surroundings; one was going to stay by the helicopter and the other would search. I could hear them on the radio calling for back-up. I knew I had to deal with these two before the back-up arrived. I

153

could see the bigger guy of the two looking at the ground for tracks.

"One person, heading that direction," he said to the other. He looked directly in my direction and started to walk towards me.

I had no choice but to leave David where he was and move. But first I covered him the best I could with some leafy fallen branches.

I watched the guy as he entered the woods. He stood metres away from David. It was due to the saving grace of the darkness and the covering that he didn't see him. He stood with his back to me, and I knew it was going to be my only chance of taking him out, but it had to be done quietly. I drew my knife from its sheath and crept towards him. I was within striking distance, when David made a sound that drew the attention of the guy to him.

He went over and started to remove the branches, but I was unable to strike as he had moved too far away. I had no choice but to rush him. As I did, the sound of breaking twigs beneath my feet warned him of my presence. As my arm came down with the knife, he grabbed my forearm. With his other hand he picked me up and threw me backwards against a tree.

With the wind taken out of me, I just laid there. The big guy stood over me smiling, then he took off his coat, exposing huge muscles, and stood his automatic gun against a tree. He took out his knife and I could see he was enjoying the prospect of killing me with it. He gestured for me to stand and pick up my knife.

As big as he was, I had no choice but to fight him.

We circled each other as he passed his knife from one hand to the other, grinning. I lunged at him and managed to draw blood from his arm, but all it did was make him smile more.

I realised he was playing with me and didn't want it to be over too quickly. I went in again, knowing his over-confidence was his weakness. As I did, I felt the sharp pain of his knife going into my side.

I dropped to my knees, unable to do anything, and resigned to the fact that this was to be my ending place. He grabbed my hair, forcing my head backwards and I saw his knife coming down towards me.

From behind him I heard a gunshot. The hand that was holding my hair went limp and a lifeless expression wiped away the smile on his face as he crumpled to the ground in front of me.

It was David - who had managed to crawl the distance, take out his gun and fire. I could see him laying there, trying to raise his head and look at me. I crawled over to him and held him in my arms. I realised he was trying to say something, so I held him closer and he said, "I had your back, my friend." With that he closed his eyes and he was gone. I knew if he had stayed where he was, he might have lived, but he sacrificed himself for me."

Johnny's eyes were brimming and he went quiet. I knew that reliving that moment was difficult and I searched for some words of comfort to help him. Then they came to me:

Greater love has no-one than this, that he lay down his life for his friends.

Yes, of course. Thank you, Lord. I spoke them to Johnny.

"Thanks, Pastor, words from the good book?"

"Yes, John 15:13."

"A great friend he was, Pastor. In fact, he was closer than a brother. Sorry about that; whenever I think about it, it makes me well up."

"Don't say sorry, Johnny; as I said, that's what I'm here for. So what happened next?"

"The sound of breaking undergrowth told me that the other guy was now coming into the woods, alerted by the gunshot.

I laid David down gently and propped my back against a tree. I knew that the more I moved, the more blood I would lose, but there was no time to do anything about it. I stayed where I was and waited for the guy to find me.

I saw the back of him, standing over his comrade. I took aim with my revolver, but the thought of shooting someone in the back - for some reason I couldn't do it.

He started to turn around and his eyes met mine. He was no more than a lad with a scared look on his face. He did nothing but froze, with my gun aiming directly at him.

My training told me that when faced with the enemy in combat, it's him or you. But, as I said, he was just a scared lad. It was as if time was in slow motion; he started to raise his automatic at me. The next thing I knew was my gun going off and the lad lying next to his comrade, dead.

He was groaning. I dragged myself over to him; he reached out and held my hand tightly and I knew he didn't have long, by the wound in his chest. As he looked into my eyes with fear, I squeezed his hand and said, "It's all right." Then his grip went limp.

I regained my senses and returned to combat mode. Not knowing how long I had before their back-up arrived, I crawled, dragging David, towards the helicopter. Where the strength came from I don't know; all I knew was I wasn't leaving him.

Managing to get him into the back of the helicopter, I got myself into the front and started the engine. I knew I had some 150 kilometres to fly before I was safe on home territory, even then - some 25k more before base.

I've got to stay awake! I kept telling myself as I could feel myself blacking out. What kept that helicopter up there was, at the time, a mystery to me but, after coming out of hospital some three weeks later, I was told that it was nothing but a miracle that I made it back. By all accounts I should have died through loss of blood long before I landed.

Afterwards, my Commander called me to his office for debriefing. He said that he noticed I had only four weeks to go before my service was up and asked what I intended to do. I told him about the flying school David and I had planned, but that now I didn't know. He told me to come and see him in four weeks; meanwhile I would be assigned a desk job on the base.

The day arrived for me to see the Commander. He informed me that I was to be awarded the Medal of Valour. Because of that, if I was interested, there would be an opportunity to train to become one of an elite special force, known as Shaldag. It would mean that I would have to sign up for another nine years, so I was told to take my time and consider it. "But remember, not many people are given the opportunity," he added. I had heard about Shaldag and to be asked to join them was the highest honour there was.

The following day I was awarded the Medal of Valour. I received it with honour, not for me but for David. I knew what I should do with it.

I had missed David's funeral, being in hospital, and hadn't spoken to his wife, Ruth, but I was told that she wanted to see me when I got out of the hospital. The reason I hadn't been to see her was that I didn't know how to face her, after failing to bring David home alive. I knew she had questions about his last moments and it was the least I could do to answer them. So I decided to go and see her.

Ruth greeted me with affection - as she normally did. I told her that David had laid down his life for me, and she said that he had told her that he would do so, if ever the need should arise. Tears were rolling down both our faces.

"Ruth," I said, "they awarded me the Medal of Valour. I don't deserve it; what David did was far braver than anything I did. I want you to have it."

She held it in her hands and cried some more. "Thank you for bringing him home," she said as we hugged.

"What will you do, now you've been discharged?" she asked.

"I've been offered the opportunity to enlist again, but I'm thinking about it," I replied.

"I think if David had had the opportunity to enlist again he would have, if he hadn't planned to start the flying school with you. But it wasn't to be. I think David would tell you to take the opportunity to enlist again."

"That's what I thought," I told her.

"Look after yourself, Yitzhak; my door is always open to you."

With that we said our goodbyes."

"And did you enlist?" I asked.

"Yes, served my nine years flying all sorts of missions, and in every one I felt David with me, having my back."

"That's some story, Johnny." I left it for a while as I could see that reliving it all had affected him. "How long before we land? And, on that subject, which airfield?"

"Well, not London - they will be waiting for us there. No, it will be somewhere small and quiet. Can you imagine landing in London with two big angels under our wings? If that didn't draw attention to us, nothing would. I haven't a clue where these guys are taking us, but I know that we can trust them. Wherever it is, it will be a safe place, and at this supersonic speed, I think we'll just have time to change back into our uniforms before we land."

As we made our way from the controls to the cabin, I felt the plane starting to descend. I looked out of the window to see that we were flying just above the water.

"What are they doing? Why are we so low?"

"So we're not detected on radar; at this level they can't see us. We must be approaching land. I'll tell you what: these guys are good - to skim the water at this speed. Take a look; we're leaving a wall of water each side of the plane."

"What speed are we doing?" I asked excitedly.

"A Learjet 85 (which this is) can fly at 545 miles an hour, but I know we're flying at least three times that speed. It's a miracle that it hasn't fallen apart."

"But that's the thing, Johnny, we're flying under the power of a miracle."

"True, Pastor, so true."

"Sir, we have just heard we lost our jet."

"What do mean, man, we lost our jet? How?"

"A missile, Sir."

"Their plane wasn't armed."

"No, Sir, it didn't come from their plane."

"If not they're plane, then whose?"

"Our plane, Sir."

"So they got away?"

"It appears so, Sir, but the last tracking position we had of them was that they were heading west, out to sea."

"They're flying to the UK. It makes sense, with them having English accents. Arrange for my plane! I'm going after them, and sort out those Bedouins!"

"Sir, they're not just Bedouins. We fired on His Royal Highness, Prince Hashem bin Al Hussein, from the House of Hashemites. They are a very powerful family. The Supreme One would not be pleased if we upset the relationship between them."

"Get my plane here fast!" he shouted.

13

Johnny was right; we barely had time to put our uniforms on, when the plane came to a gentle halt.

"We're down, Pastor. I couldn't have landed it better myself."

"The little I know about planes, you could put on a postage stamp, but I do know you couldn't have landed it, especially without a tail."

"Yeah, I suppose you've got a small point there."

"Small!"

"What do you want me to say, I couldn't land it?"

"Well, it would be a start."

"You change your tune; one minute you're calling me superhuman, and now...."

"Can we get off this plane? I'm dying to know where we are; we can finish this later."

"Sure, Pastor. I've been waiting for *you*."

The first thing I did when my feet stepped onto the ground was to look and see if Mordecai and Aquila were still with us. To my delight they were, but greatly reduced in size than they were while flying the plane with the wings in their hands.

Mordecai was standing in a majestic pose with his gold armour and sword, and Aquila with her long, golden hair and headband, was beside him in her armour with a gold staff.

"I hope you enjoyed the flight?" said Mordecai.

In his humorous way, Johnny replied, "Yes, it was nearly as good as if I was flying the plane."

"Johnny!"

"What?"

"You are speaking to an angel."

"Mordecai knows I'm joking; we go back some way."

"I make allowances for him, Pastor. If he wasn't so important to the plan, I would squash him."

The grin on Johnny's face disappeared.

"Even angels can joke," Mordecai said.

"Hello, Christian, we meet again."

"Yes, Smiley, I had a feeling you'd been with me all along."

She smiled. "That is true. Because I've been assigned to you, Christian, I will always will be with you."

"Where are we?" I asked them.

"You're south of Edinburgh; it's a disused World War 2 airfield. In the hangar over there, Johnny, you will find transport to your liking, and a change of clothes. I've also entered new ID chips into your device.

"Why so far from London? Couldn't you have snapped your fingers and caused us to materialise at home, like some of the testimonies I've heard from people?"

"Yes, I could have - but your assignment hasn't finished. Your journey south is part of it, Johnny.

Now you must go, there is a person waiting for your help."

"Well, Pastor, you'll just have to keep your promise to Linda waiting a little longer," Johnny said, turning to me.

"I'm in the Lord's hands and if He still has some use for me, then so be it. I will get home in his timing."

Johnny turned to speak to Mordecai but he and Aquila had gone.

"He always does that - leaving me with unanswered questions!" Johnny said in frustration.

"What question did you have for him?"

"Like, what's this persons name?"

"*All that you need to know at the moment is in the car, the rest will be revealed when it's needed,*" boomed back.

"Looks like you got your answer, Johnny."

"That was an answer? Well, I suppose it will have to do. Well, Pastor, it looks as if we're on another adventure!"

As we opened back the huge steel hangar doors, there before us was an old Bentley.

"I can't believe it. Do you know what we have here, Pastor?"

"A Bentley?"

"So, you know your cars then?"

"No, but I guess by the name 'Bentley' on the grill, that's what it is?"

"Ah, yes, but do you know what model it is?"

"I already told you I don't know about cars. Something tells me I'm going to have another history lesson - about vintage cars, whether I like it or not."

163

"Pastor, you've got to let me tell you about this; it's a subject I'm passionate about. As for *this* car, I don't know where to start. I saw it race once – and I thought at the time how much I'd love to drive it, and now I've got the desire of my heart."

"The quicker we get it over with, the quicker we can get going and the quicker I get home, so please start!"

"This is a Bentley Meteor, powered by a Rolls-Royce 27-litre V-12 from a Spitfire fighter. While Bentley never actually produced a car like the Meteor, it was built to compete in a contest against the German car, powered by a Heinkel He 111 bomber engine (the Brutus). They called it the 'Battle of Britain'. This 19-ft baby pushes out 850 horsepower, theoretically capable of reaching 160 miles an hour."

"What that old thing does 160 miles an hour?"

"It was built to resemble a vintage pre-war Bentley; don't worry, Pastor, we won't be doing anything near that. There's only one problem: although the fuel tank holds 105 gallons, it's a thirsty beast, delivering just 3 miles a gallon."

"Couldn't Mordecai have found something a little more economical and less conspicuous?"

"The way I see it (putting the economy to one side): who would think that two guys being searched for would drive around in something like this, that would only draw attention to them? No, I understand Mordecai's logic."

"So did it win?"

"It sure did."

While he was giving me the history of the car, I was curious to see what was in the two brown parcels on the seat. "Have you seen these clothes that I assume we have to put on?"

"No, Pastor. I was too engrossed talking and looking at the car. What have we got then? Oh, yes! Vintage clothes to match, with leather helmets and goggles - but there are three sets; who's the other set for?"

"I haven't got a clue. I didn't supply them. Ask Mordecai."

"Maybe I'll do just that. Who's the other set of clothes for, Mordecai?"

"*For a person to come*," came back the answer.

"Fantastic. Thanks, Mordecai - that answered a lot."

"*You're welcome*," came back.

Dressed in our tweed outfits with helmets, we got into the car.

"So what does it say?" I said, as Johnny read the paper; who are we supposed to be?"

"Oh, I just love this: we work for State TV, involved with making a documentary on classic cars. We're film producers. You're 'Charles Goodwood' and I'm 'Peter Pearson', Senior Director."

"That figures," I said watching Johnny put on his goggles.

"Ready, Pastor, for the ride of your life? You might want to put on your goggles."

As Johnny pushed the button on the ignition, the mighty engine let out a roar and, with lightning acceleration, we left the hangar.

"I'm intrigued to know more about the mission. Do you think this car has something to do with it?" I shouted, trying to make him hear above the noise of the engine.

I didn't get an answer; I could see he was lost in the excitement of the car. The trees and bushes each side of the narrow winding lanes were flashing by at great speed as we headed south. It was a miracle that we didn't meet anything coming the other way. I knew the 19 ft monster was built for speed (as I was experiencing) but not about its brakes, which I was just about to find out.

We came to a screeching halt.

"What's up?" I asked.

"We've missed our turning, back there."

"I thought you didn't know where we were going?"

"I don't, but I had a strong feeling we should have turned left back there."

"Then we'd better follow your strong feeling."

As the lane was too narrow to turn around, Johnny reversed the car until we came to the turning. I thought the lane we were on was narrow, but this was no more than a single dirt track. Slowly we made our way along it, occasionally bottoming the car on the bumps. We had been travelling for about twenty minutes, when we came into a clearing. Ahead of us was a rundown wooden building.

"What do you think, Pastor?" Johnny said, stopping the car.

"Well, it's a bit late to ask that; if there is anyone around, they sure know we're here - with the amount of noise this car makes. They probably heard us coming from way back."

"Well, there's only one way to find out if this is where we're supposed to be."

166

"That's the problem, Johnny; we don't know. All we have is your 'strong feeling'."

"Well, it hasn't let us down so far," he said with one of his annoying chuckles.

As we pulled up outside the building, I was sure I caught a glimpse of someone in the window looking from behind a curtain.

"I think there's someone in, Johnny."

"Yeah, I saw him."

We got out of the car and headed for the door and were just about to knock. The door was cautiously opened a little way and, from behind it, a man's head appeared.

"Are you lost?" he said.

"We're not sure, but I think we're supposed to be here."

He gave us a suspicious look as he glanced over at the car. "Who are you looking for?" he asked.

"Douglas McDougal," Johnny replied.

"Who is it that wants him?"

"Peter Pearson and Charles Goodwood," Johnny said.

He went quiet and his face looked mystified. "You'd better come in," he said, opening the door fully, and ushering us in. "Please sit down."

He sat down opposite and looked at each of our faces. I sensed by the look on his face he wasn't sure whether he should say something or not.

"I know you don't know us, and you have to be extra careful about what you say, and to whom, these days but I just want you to know you can trust us, Mr McDougal."

"I didn't say I'm McDougal."

"No, you didn't; are you?" Johnny said.

167

There was silence, then he said, "Okay. I've got a feeling that I can trust you. You're not going to believe what I'm about to tell you. Some weeks ago, the Lord spoke to me and said that He wanted me to tell the people that He was about to return. I said that, as He knew, I'd been secretly telling people in Edinburgh. But He said, "I want you to go on television and tell them."

You can imagine what I said. "But how?' I wouldn't know where to start, especially as the State has strict control over the airway and what's said. So, to speak about God would be impossible and, if he wanted me to do it, He would have to send me the help I would need. Then last night the Lord spoke two names to me. They were your names."

"That sounds like Him," Johnny remarked.

"So tell me, Mr McDougal, what are you doing out here in such a remote place?" I asked.

He looked a lot more relaxed as he said, "Please, call me Douglas. I had to get out of Edinburgh a bit quick, as word came to me that the State police were on to me for preaching the Word. One of my friends was left this place and said that I could stay here. He assured me that no one knew of the place; and that was a year ago. He's the only person I see, when he brings supplies. You two are a most welcome answer to prayer."

"So, getting His Word on television is the purpose of our mission?"

"It looks like that, Pastor," Johnny remarked.

"Pastor? You called him Pastor?" Douglas said surprised.

"Sorry, Pastor, it just came out."

"That's okay, Johnny. I don't think we'll have any problems with Douglas."

"So I take it Peter Pearson and Charles Goodwood
 are not your real names?"

"No, but I'm sure you understand these times demand caution," I said.

"Oh, absolutely."

"Is Douglas McDougal *your* real name?"

"Aye, there's no need to say otherwise now - and I don't see anyone out here. So you say 'mission'? Who are you guys? Who sent you?"

"The same person who told you what He wants you to do and gave you *our* names," I replied.

"Praise the Lord. It's so good to be in the company of fellow believers again; I've missed it for so long. So what's with the outfits and the car?"

"We didn't get a say on that. All we know, at this stage, is that we're film producers making a documentary on classic cars," Johnny said with a chuckle, "and what that has to do with God's Word, your guess is as good as mine, Douglas; but knowing Him . . . "

"His thoughts are not our thoughts," I interrupted.

"Well, it sounds as if it's going to be a way of getting God's word on television. I'm sure, when the time is right, it will all fit into place," Johnny concluded.

"You guys hungry?"

"I thought you'd never ask," Johnny replied.

As Douglas went off to prepare some food, I asked Johnny, "Was it Mordecai who told you Douglas's name?"

"When I hear voices in my head, I take it for granted it's him; after all, he said he'd be with me on my missions."

"Thank God he is."

"Amen there, Pastor."

Sitting around the table we discussed further details of the plan.

"So where actually are we, Douglas?"

"Just outside Crieff, Pastor."

Johnny looked on his pad. "According to this, there is a television broadcasting studio just outside Edinburgh, at a place called Inverkeithing."

"I heard there was going to be a new studio, but I didn't think it was on air yet; mind you, that was a year ago, so it might be up and running now," Douglas said.

"Well, according to this, it is, so it looks like that's where we have to get you, Douglas. You're going to need a new identity; now what name shall we give you?"

"What? You can do that?"

"Douglas, trust me, this man can do almost anything," I told him.

"There's just one thing: with you two dressed like that, I'll stand out like a sore thumb."

Johnny and I smiled at each other and said in unison, "The third set of clothes?"

"We leave in the morning," Johnny announced.

14

"**A**re you okay, Douglas - not too windy back there?"

"No, I'm quite enjoying it; you'll have to tell me how you came across this car," he shouted.

"Long story," Johnny hollered back.

The monster of a car roared along, drawing attention from the people we passed as we headed for the studio.

It wasn't long before we drew up at the car park barrier.

Seeing there were two armed guards standing there, I said, "What now, Johnny? I assume we've got some valid papers to get in there?"

"Not at the moment, Pastor, but I'm sure that when that security guy looks at them, they will be in order."

"Of course they will. I forgot for the moment - when we need it, it will appear."

"That's the ticket, Pastor."

"I wouldn't have thought that this small studio in the middle of nowhere would warrant armed guards."

"Yes, even up here, Pastor, especially with broadcasting stations. The State would not want to take any chances of anything they don't approve of getting on the airways and television."

"What was it you two were talking about earlier, to do with the papers? Do you mind telling me?" Douglas asked.

"Not enough time to explain, Douglas; just trust us."

"Good morning, documents please," said the guy at the barrier. After scrutinising them, he said, "Thank you, sir; that's fine."

As the barrier rose we drove through. The 19 ft monster took up two parking bays.

"Right gentlemen, don't forget who we are."

"Remind me."

"Duncan Drummond," Johnny said, "our narrator."

"Thinking about it, I don't know anything about classic cars," Douglas said with a note of apprehension in his voice.

"I'm sure, the minute you open your mouth, the Lord will give you the words."

"Thanks for the reassurance, Pastor."

"He's good at that," Johnny said. "Right, no more using our real names; let me do all the talking."

We approached the reception desk and sitting there was a ginger-haired woman.

"Yes, gentleman, how can we help you?"

"Mr Cameron is expecting us," Johnny replied.

"Your names?"

"Peter Pearson, Charles Goodwood and Duncan Drummond. We're here to make a documentary."

She picked up the phone, "Mr Cameron, there are some gentleman here to see you. Please take a seat; he's on his way down."

"Mordecai again?" I asked.

"No.   When I looked up the studio I saw his name, he's the Director."

"Gentleman, welcome. I've been expecting you. I must say, I'm quite excited about your documentary, and to have such well-known producers here. It's been a long time since we've had anything like this. Shall we go up to my office?"

We followed him up to his plush office and drew up chairs around his huge desk.

Turning around in his swivel chair and looking out of the window to the car park below, he said, "So is that the famous Bentley Meteor? I had to see what the noise was in the car park when you came in. I recognised the car straight away. I had the privilege to be at the filming of the race, when I worked for the BBC. That car won me a bit of money - I had a wager on it to win. My only regret was that I didn't get a chance to ride in it. When this is over, any chance of a ride?"

"I'm sure that can be arranged, Mr Cameron," Johnny replied.

"So, Mr Pearson, the studio has been made ready for you; the crew are at your disposal. Bruce is on his way up to take you there. If there's anything you need, please don't hesitate to let me know."

"That's kind of you, Mr Cameron, but I think we have all we need. I must say, your organisation is very efficient, in that you knew of our arrival. I'm used to having to explain that we had an appointment."

173

I could see that Johnny was intrigued, as much as I was, as to how he knew we were coming, although I suspected that there was an element of supernatural at work.

"I must confess, I owe my efficiency to my secretary; she's one in a million. Funnily enough, your appointment was a little bit of a mystery. She told me that she couldn't remember entering it on the computer but it sort of appeared there. She joked about it and said that I must have been working her too hard. (As if I would!)

Anyway, Gentlemen, I'll leave you in the hands of Bruce. By the way, I love your outfits - a nice touch."

We followed Bruce to the studio, not knowing how we were going to pull this off. Bruce and the team waited for our instructions.

"I was told that you were shooting a documentary about classic cars so I took the liberty of putting that backdrop of old cars up. Will that be okay or would you like something else?" Bruce ventured.

"No, that's fine, it will do just fine. I think we have all we need; we'll be doing a single take, so it will be going out live, will it not?" Johnny said to him.

"Well … usually it's pre-recorded then approved. I'll check with the powers-that-be, upstairs."

"Bruce, it's the only way I work. It's that or not at all. We're on a tight schedule and I've allocated only a short amount of time here. We've got another shoot to do, far south. So, if you want to be the one to tell Mr Cameron that you were the reason his studio didn't get used for this special event, then please do."

Johnny was playing his authority card to the full and I could see by the look on Bruce's face that he was in a huge dilemma.

"I'm sure, Mr Pearson, this time it will be okay; it's just that nowadays there's so much protocol and paperwork to follow, but with you being such a famous producer, maybe we can waive all that."

"Good, now if we could be left alone?"

"Of course. I'll be on the other side of the glass; I'll give you your cue when to start. Let me know if you need anything."

"Okay, Duncan, the floor's all yours."

'Duncan' stood in front of the backdrop and waited for the cue from Bruce. With a show of fingers counting down from three, Duncan started.

"There is something special about the enthusiast who owns a classic-car. You only have to listen to them talk about it. They have a passion, a love, a *want* to be involved in owning such a vehicle, and especially in its restoration.

Once it is made, all shining and in mint condition, in the factory, it goes on a journey. Much depends on who owns it.

It could be a loving, careful owner, giving it all the attention it needs; an owner who would cherish it and keep it away from any harsh conditions that would harm it.

However, sometimes it's subject to careless ownership, which ultimately can lead to it becoming a wreck on a scrapheap.

But if it does, as in life, there is always the hope of restoration for the car and, in the right hands, it can be brought back from a broken-down heap to pristine condition, looking new and even better than before. And why? *Because of the love for it.* After it's restored there will always be a story to tell by the

175

new owner, who stands there proud of the restoration he has done on it.

A true enthusiast will not stop at one abandoned car. Because of the passion and love for them, they will go about, scouring the dark and rundown places where they have been abandoned, rescuing them. That's the love affair with the classic car.

And, like the classic car enthusiast, we have someone who has a love affair with us, who is passionate about us, so much so that He doesn't want us to end up on the scrapheap of life. When He made us, we were in pristine condition, we were cared for - His pride and joy. But, unfortunately most of us were easily led and subject to reckless behaviour, leading to destruction. But His grace and mercy is poured out on us (like the car), restoring us to the former glory of how He intended us to be.

Because He has so much love for us and so much compassion, Jesus is coming again to give us another chance to accept him. He has already been (not long ago) to collect those who had already said 'yes' to Him.

The State told us that aliens were the reason for the disappearance of so many people. But I've been sent to tell you the truth. He is coming very soon. If you don't want to end up on that scrapheap, be ready for Him and say: "Yes, I need you Lord". Let Him find you and, like the classic car, let Him restore you."

Halfway through Duncan's monologue, Bruce was frantically pushing buttons on the security lock, trying to get into the room; but Johnny had already changed the combination when he closed the door. It was obvious, from Bruce's lips behind the glass screen, the word: 'Cut!' was being shouted at the guys on the sound desk.

Then, in the sound room, he was frantically pulling cables out of their sockets, and still God's word was being broadcasted.

"Throw the mains switch!" he shouted at the technician, in order to cut all power to the studio. He was obeyed immediately but nothing happened.

"That's impossible!" Bruce yelled. The technicians looked at each other, shrugging their shoulders, unable to shut it down.

Outside the door appeared the Director, Mr Cameron, and two armed guards, who obediently began trying to get in.

"Well, Johnny, any ideas about this one?" I asked him.

"You're the Pastor. Do what you do best."

"And what's that?"

"Pray!"

Johnny went over to the window. "Too far to jump," he announced. It's down to you, Pastor."

"No pressure then. Lord, a little help here please. The possibility of us getting out of here in one piece looks hopeless, but I know that with you all things are possible. So we hand it over to you."

The room filled with a blinding flash and before us stood Mordecai and Aquila in all their glory.

"You've got yourself into another pickle, Johnny. It looks as though we're going to have to get you out of it again."

"What do mean: '*I got myself into*'? It was you who assigned me to this mission."

"We'll discuss it later, Johnny, after we get you out," Mordecai replied.

I forgot Duncan was in the room. When I looked over, he was standing there gazing at these two supernatural beings with a look of fear and amazement.

"They're on our side, Duncan. I was the same when I first saw them; it's reassuring that they're here for us in times like this."

Duncan didn't say a word; he just continued to stare in awe.

"Aren't you going to strike them down so we can get out of here, Mordecai?"

"No, Johnny, there's no need. The flash of light has temporarily blinded them - you can walk past them whenever you're ready. Speak to you soon."

As usual, the two disappeared as quickly as they came.

Outside the door, everyone was fumbling around in their blindness. We silently walked right past them and made our way down to reception.

"How did it go?" enquired the ginger-haired woman behind the desk.

"It was a blinder," replied Johnny with a smile. "I didn't get a chance to thank Mr Cameron. Would you tell him it was a pleasure using his facilities. Oh, I nearly forgot: tell him sorry about not giving him a ride; maybe next time. Bye!"

We climbed into the Meteor and, with a roar, we left the place.

"This is HQ London. What's going on up there, Edinburgh? This monstrous dirge you have allowed is being broadcasted on all monitors throughout every city. Shut it down *now*!"

"We have located it to a small studio in Inverkeithing; our troops are on their way, as we speak."

Officer Shorts, who was now in the London HQ, said: "You'll recall we had a similar situation in Jerusalem a little while ago; I think the two that I followed here are responsible for this as well."

"Are their faces on the system?"

"No; they have evaded all cameras so far, but I've had a rough sketch of them drawn up from memory. Put it on the facial recognition system - it might pull up one or two main features that will be enough to identify them."

"Consider it done."

"I'll take charge of this – I have a personal interest in these two."

"Our division is at your disposal; take as many men as you like with you."

"I normally only take two with me, as long as they're big."

"I've got just the two for you. When do you want to leave?"

The London HQ Commander couldn't help but stifle a smirk as he pictured the little officer with the two huge guards that he had in mind.

"I'll need a room with a desk and virtual maps of the area up there; I need to study the routes they will be thinking of taking to get away."

"I'll get it arranged, and have the two men assigned to you when you're ready to leave."

As he sat at his desk he started to speak out loud. "Now you two, I've got a feeling you're going to make your way here. You're not stupid enough to try to cover the whole distance by car and you will stay away from towns and cities because of the surveillance cameras. But that hasn't stopped you before.

Somehow you've fooled the system by changing your IDs. Let's hope your desperation to get away causes you to make a mistake - and when you do . .

Now let's see. Train! Maybe not, that would mean exposure to cameras at the station and on the trains, but it's the safest and fastest way of travelling. I think you will take the risk.

So where will you get on? Of course: Manchester to London train. Providing it's non-stop, I'll be waiting for you at the station; there will be no escaping me this time!"

He went back into the Command Centre office and said to the Commander, "We need to have all the Manchester to London trains running non-stop till they get to London. I've a feeling my two low-lifes will be on one of them."

"That shouldn't be a problem. I'll get someone to see to it. I take it you'll be at the station waiting for them?"

"Yes, I'll be leaving now, if you could arrange for a car and my two men?"

The Commander didn't like the thought of some other officer (especially from another country) taking the credit for capturing the two. Calling his second-in-command into his office, he said: "Forget that last order. What men do we have around about here?" he said, pointing to a wall map.

"We have a squad in training in the Valley Park, Sir."

"Hmm, it looks as if the train passes by there. Stop all trains there and have some of those men search them. When you find the two, I want them brought here. Is that clear? Yes, this will go very well for me - maybe a promotion."

15

We were soon back at Duncan's place with smug looks on our faces, knowing we had triumphed again over the enemy.

"Do you think it's still being transmitted?" Duncan asked.

"Well, if it's anything like the discs in Jerusalem, I would think so. As the place is away from the city, it will take them time to get there, and then they have to find a way to shut it down, so I would say: yes." Johnny answered him.

"So you've done this before? Who *are* you two?" Duncan asked us.

"We're just two normal guys like you, Duncan, being used by the Lord," I said.

"I wouldn't say 'normal'. It's not every day that two big angels materialise in front of you! No, that's not normal," he replied.

"Duncan, when you do the Lord's work, trust me - it's normal," Johnny remarked.

"So what's next for you two?"

"Well, I'd like to say home, but that's not for us to decide. We could end up anywhere. Can we stay the night? Hopefully, by morning, we might know whether we're going home or not."

"Sure, Pastor; it's the least I can do for helping me to do the Lord's bidding."

The morning came without anything from the Lord about a new assignment.

"Duncan, do you have any form of transport here and any old clothes we can change into?" Johnny asked.

"Only an old pickup truck in the barn, but I'm not sure if it will start. It was here when I came, so I don't know how long it is since it's been started. Why do you ask?"

"I don't think we'll get far in these clothes and the car. The Meteor (as much as I love it) has served its purpose of convincing them about the documentary. No, if we want to get far, it's going to have to stay here in your barn, and we'll take the truck - if that's okay with you."

"I've no need for any fancy clothes so there's nothing much, but if you're happy wearing dungarees – yes, and if you can get it started, you're welcome; but be aware there won't be any record of it on the system. So if you were caught on one of those monitors or stopped . . ."

"Don't worry about that - it's a minor detail. Maybe, after coffee I'll have a go at getting it started."

When Johnny had finished his coffee, he changed into the dungarees and went outside.

184

"That Johnny, he's a resourceful fellow! Is there anything he can't do?"

"I told you he could do almost anything."

Outside there was the whine of an engine turning over and then a bang, followed by a cloud of smoke and an engine starting.

"He got it going then."

"I had no doubt that he would."

After I'd changed, Duncan and I went outside; there was Johnny at the wheel of the truck with a smug look on his face.

"The Meteor *just* fitted in the barn, Duncan; the keys are in it, if you want to use it, but I would resist it for a while - until it all dies down out there."

"As tempting as it is, I'll give it a miss. So what do you want me to do with it?"

"Do what you like with it - it's yours. Let's just say it's a little parting gift."

"It's not so little, Johnny," Duncan replied.

"I suppose not. You ready to go home, Pastor?"

"Is this going to get us home?" I asked, as it shook the life out of me with every bump in the road.

"I'm sure it will get us a fair distance - if it doesn't pack up, and if it does, we still have an option."

"And that is?"

"We walk."

"Not the option I was looking for."

"Just joking, something will turn up."

"I've just had a thought; what about our new IDs and the truck?"

185

"You've got a point there, Pastor. We'll pull over as soon as we can, while we're away from any towns."

It wasn't long before we pulled of the road into a track leading into a wood.

"So we need something that ties up with these dungarees and the truck; what do you think: builders?"

"Anyone could tell by looking at my hands that I'm not a builder."

He ferreted in the glove box and said, "Here, put these on."

"How did you know there were gloves in there?"

"It's a glove box isn't it?" he chuckled. "So, you are: 'Stanley Watson, labourer', and I will be: 'Michael Manson, Director of Manson Builders' and the truck is . . . registered in the company name. There, all done," he said, pushing the button on his pad.

"Why is it, every time we have new IDs, you are either my superior or my boss?"

"When we rescued Linda, you were the officer weren't you?"

"Well I suppose I was, but there's still an imbalance here."

"I'll tell you what, if it makes you feel better, and if there's a next time, I'll make you the boss. How's that?"

"Don't bother, let's just get going."

"Okay, Pastor Grumpy."

"Did you say something, Johnny?"

"I said: 'The road's very bumpy'."

We had travelled about 100 miles, deliberately avoiding any built up areas, but we hadn't come across a filling station and were in need of fuel. We had no choice but to pass through the town that was ahead.

We stopped at the first fuel station we came to. The first thing I noticed was the monitoring camera turning towards us.

"Don't say anything, just look relaxed," Johnny said, getting out to put fuel in. "I'll see if they have anything to eat at the counter; I won't be long."

I was looking at Johnny through the glass of the shop, when I caught the eye of a guy looking over. I turned away, pretending I hadn't seen him. When I turned back, he wasn't there.

Suddenly there was a tap on my window. I turned and there was a man staring intently at me. The way he stood and the look on his face told me he was obviously State personnel. He directed me to wind down my window.

"You don't see many of these old petrol things nowadays. Mind if I have a look under the bonnet?"

"No . . . I'll try and release it," I said. Looking under the dash, I had no idea where the lever was. "Sorry, I'm having trouble finding the lever. The truck's not mine, it's my boss's. He's getting some food." I was hoping he'd say, "Okay, don't worry", and go, but he said, "I'll wait."

To my relief, Johnny came back.

"Can I help you?" Johnny asked him.

"I was asking your friend here if I could have a peep under the bonnet; it's so rare to see one of these, what with all the electric cars on the road."

"Yeah, sure."

Johnny instantly knew where the lever was. As he lifted it, there was a rusty, creaking sound.

"Pre-nineties?" he asked.

"You know your cars; to be precise, 1989."

"And still going? Cars aren't made like that nowadays. It's all throwaway parts now. By the look of the dust under here, you'd think it's been off the road for years."

"No, it's used every day for work," Johnny assured him.

"So where are you heading?"

"Manchester, to look at a building job."

"Is it reliable enough to get you that far?"

"Yeah - it's never let me down; I've travelled miles in the old rust bucket."

"Well, good luck with that; as much as I love old cars, I certainly wouldn't drive that far."

Johnny closed the bonnet and got back in. The guy gave us a half-hearted wave and we drove off.

"That was close! Can't we just drive something a little in keeping, so we don't draw attention to ourselves?"

"I think it's the Lord's way of showing us that, even when things get a bit intense, He's there for us."

"You're probably right, Johnny. And, on the subject of the Lord, I think you owe Him a few apologies for telling whoppers."

"Yeah, yeah, I know - but I had to think of something quick."

"But I'll to give it to you, you certainly know your vehicles - giving him the precise year of it."

"I would agree with you and say I'm brilliant, but it was an educated guess, based on the registration. I could have been a year out either way, but I'm pretty confident he didn't know for sure."

"One day, Johnny, your cap's not going to fit your head."

"Pastor, I don't know what you mean."

We were just a few miles from Manchester when the truck's engine started to display steam from under the bonnet.

"Looks like it's the end of the road for the old rust bucket, Pastor."

"Well, I suppose we've got to be thankful it got us this far."

"Yep! It's time to stretch your legs."

We ditched the truck on the grass verge and started walking.

"I wonder what's waiting for us up ahead."

"Hopefully nothing, Pastor, but then you never know if Mordecai will appear with something else to do. You can't help wondering whether the old truck broke down for a purpose, or it was just that the engine gave up through high mileage."

"Half of me doesn't mind if He did make it break down for a purpose, and the other half feels that it would be nice to go home."

"I know what you mean, Pastor; I must confess this is the longest assignment that I've been on. Yes, it would be nice."

"You'll have to find us some transport, Johnny."

"Why me?"

"Well, you're the boss, Mr Manson."

"You're definitely in charge next time, Mr Watson."

I hadn't been to Manchester for many years; the last time I was there was for a large Christian conference. The city had changed beyond recognition with its new towering buildings and overhead rail system. Like London, there were cameras and listening terminals positioned everywhere. I couldn't help noticing that the people seemed to have a look of fear on their faces. Controlled puppets came to mind.

Aware of all the monitoring, I made sure I didn't use the wrong name when speaking to Johnny.

"In between the listening points, I said, "Michael, do you notice anything about the people?"

"What the puppet syndrome?"

"That's the same word that came to me; it seems worse up here than London."

"I think this was one of the first places they tried out the new systems of control on the people and they've had more time to perfect it than in the other cities."

"Won't we stand out like a sore thumb here?"

"How are your acting skills, Mr Watson?"

Because we were approaching another listening point, we didn't say anything, we just walked imitating the look of the people.

"I think we should get out of this place as soon as we can. Have you come up with any ideas yet?"

"I'm working on it, Mr Watson. Train?"

"Mr Manson, I don't care if it's a horse and cart, if it means we get out of here."

"I thought you said you didn't want any more transport that drew attention to us."

"Train will be fine. Which way?"

I thought the main centre was bad enough with all the cameras, but the station had three times as many, plus armed guards at the entrance as well as the platforms.

As we entered the station there seemed to be some kind of disturbance between the guards and the crowds of people, who were looking up at a huge TV screen.

And there was Duncan, telling the people to repent as the Lord was coming back soon. The pair of us had to restrain ourselves from laughing.

Even with all the commotion and security, we had no trouble getting clearance or boarding the train for London, apart from being asked what our purpose for travelling was, and Johnny satisfied them with his answer.

As we took our seats in the carriage, I noticed cameras even there. There was an unusual silence among the passengers. No one was talking or even looking around. It wasn't normal for people to behave like that. Even the children weren't behaving like children; there wasn't even a giggle from them; they had the same puppet-like look as the adults.

The train moved out of the station and was soon up to speed.

I must have shut my eyes for what seemed a few minutes, when the train came to a jolting halt.

"Time to move, Mr Watson," announced Johnny.

Being a little disorientated, I said, "What's up?"

"Security guards have just got on. I have a feeling they're looking for us."

"What? How could they know we're on the train?"

"All I can think of is facial recognition from the cameras."

"Are you sure it's us they're looking for?"

"Do you want to take the chance? Trust me, we move."

"But there's nowhere to go; if you remember we're on a train."

"If we don't get off now we're not going to, once it gets moving again. Now, follow me and keep your head down."

The guards had got on at the front and were working their way back. We made our way from one carriage to the other until we were at the rear.

"The doors are locked! Do something with your gizmo, Johnny!"

"Don't panic, it's all under control."

I looked through the adjoining carriage window.

"Johnny, they're coming!"

I felt a jolt as the train started to move. I looked at Johnny and could see that, for some reason, he was having trouble trying to open the doors. The guards had finished checking everyone in the next carriage and were about to enter ours. I'm sure the Lord loves me saying His name. In desperation, from my lips came the word: "Jesus!"

With a beep the doors slid open.

"Jump!" Johnny said.

The train had picked up momentum but I knew there was no time for hesitation. I leapt and felt the embankment stones tear into the skin on my back as I slid down it. Thinking Johnny was behind me, I looked up to see him hanging on the outside of the train, trying to fiddle with his gizmo as the train went further away.

Why aren't you jumping? I said under my breath. I could see that whatever Johnny was doing had put his life in danger if he jumped, as the train was now moving at great speed.

"Lord, don't let him hurt himself. Protect him as he jumps," I prayed.

Johnny leapt from the train and, although he was some distance away, I couldn't mistake what I was seeing. It was as if someone invisible had caught him and gently lowered him to the ground. I ran as fast as I could to get to him.

Johnny was just sitting there.

"You okay?"

"Give me a mo, Pastor; I'm trying to understand what just happened. At that speed, there was very little chance of me making it, but I felt a sensation of floating when I jumped off."

"That's what I saw. You did! You literally floated to the ground. God came through for you, Johnny. I thought you were behind me. What were you doing? Why didn't you jump when I did?"

"I had to buy us some time. I jammed the doors closed to stop them coming after us. By the time they get them open, they'll be a long way down the track. Give us a hand up. We'd better get moving."

"Any idea where we are?" I asked.

"I noticed that unscheduled stop where the guards got on was in the middle of some valley regional park. Why they didn't leave it until we got to London doesn't make sense - unless they had them in the area for some reason."

"So I take it we're still in the park?" I asked.

"Yes, and we can use that to our advantage, as there won't be any cameras."

"Is this place big?"

"If it's the place I think it is, about 40 square miles, with plenty of places to lose ourselves. We stand a chance of getting home, providing we stay away from the Visitors' Centre."

"What's wrong with the Visitors' Centre? We can get food and drink there can't we?"

"No, they'll have cameras, and there are bound to be guards there by now; that's why we stay well clear."

"So how far is home from here?"

"Not far, 14 or 15 miles by road, but they'll have every exit of this park closed off by now."

"So how are we going to get out of here then?"

"While we were on the train I noticed a canal and it goes right through the park. That's our way out. In theory it should take us all the way into London. Hopefully they haven't got the waterways covered. You fit, Pastor?"

"Ready when you are, Johnny."

As we cautiously made our way through the park, I couldn't help thinking how Linda would have loved it here with its meandering footpaths threading through the woods, filled with wild flowers and streams. I was brought back to reality by Johnny's voice.

"There it is," he announced.

As we came to the edge of the trees, there in front of us was the canal. I was about to walk over to it when:

"Wait! Let me check there's no one on the path."

Johnny cautiously made his way out from the trees, looking left and right.

"It's clear, but we'll stay under cover of the trees as far as we can. You never know who's on this path."

"So how do you propose we get a boat: flag one down, hijack it?"

"Trust me, Pastor, we'll get one."

"There's that 'trust me' again."

194

"Did you say something, Pastor?"

I could see why Johnny had made the decision to keep off the footpath, as a helicopter passed low over the top of the trees.

"Looks like they're determined to find us; I pray there's a boat ahead soon."

"You know, Pastor, I've been thinking about all this activity, trying to get us. It can't be because of the television studio episode."

"Why not? That's the only problem we've caused for them since we've been back in the country."

"No, it's since we entered Manchester Station, and I think we got scanned by the cameras. It had to be that, as I disabled the cameras at the studio, which means our faces wouldn't be recognised on the system. Also, they'd be looking for a group of three, if it was merely over that."

"So you're saying they were looking for us before?"

"I think you hit the nail on the head when you said 'since we've been back in the country'. I've got a feeling The Squirt is behind this – he's the only one that would recognise us."

"What! You think he followed us to the UK?"

"It has to be it."

"But how could he know we came to the UK?"

"I reckon they must have tracked the plane."

"I can't believe he's that determined to find us. Are you sure it's him?"

"Not a hundred percent, but it's the only explanation I can think of for all this activity. If it *is* him, he's in London, probably at the station - hoping that we'll be delivered into his hands. But I reckon someone has slipped up by stopping the train before it got to London. I reckon he's pacing up and down that platform screaming at everyone for letting us escape."

"I wouldn't like to be those guards on the train when they tell him we got away. I almost feel sorry for them."

"Only you could come out with something like that, Pastor. Do you think he's grown since we last saw him?"

"What? Trust you to come out with something like that. Although he might have taller guards."

"Look! There's the answer to your prayers, Pastor."

And there moored at the embankment was a long boat that appeared to have nobody on it.

"What do you think, Johnny?"

"I think we wait a while; there could be someone inside the cabin, or they might have moored up and gone for a walk, which is very likely."

"Don't people who use these canals moor their barge and trek to a pub?"

"I don't think so with this boat - there isn't a pub for miles. As I said, we'll wait a while, then make our move."

"What, we're just going to take it? Wouldn't that be stealing?"

"I wouldn't go as far as to say 'stealing', more 'borrowing' it, Pastor."

"Is that supposed to make me feel better?"

"Look, now's not the time to debate the issue. It's either borrow the boat or be caught, and I know which I'm choosing."

"Okay, okay but it goes against my conscience."

We waited for some time and, as there appeared to be no movement on the boat, it seemed that nobody was on board.

"You know, Pastor, I've been thinking: that boat has either been abandoned (which would be strange) or the Lord has answered your prayers again, by putting it there. What do you think?"

"I'd say the latter."

"Yeah, I'm inclined to agree with you."

Johnny made sure once again that the footpath was clear, then we went to the boat.

"You deal with the mooring line, Pastor, and I'll get the engine started."

The engine started making its chugging sound and we were soon moving slowly down the canal. I ventured down to the cabin.

"See if there's any food in there, Pastor," Johnny called.

There was everything for a three-course meal and even the table had been laid out for two. *Thank you, Lord, I know now this is of you.* And, when I walked into the other room, there was the confirmation. Laid out on the bed were two sets of men's clothes.

"Johnny, you're not going to believe this! Not only is they're enough food here to feed us for a week, but a change of clothes and they look the right size. How amazing it that?"

"Sounds like it was the Lord."

I changed clothes and ate some food then took over from Johnny. I was most impressed with myself, as I had never steered a boat before.

Johnny, having eaten and changed, came back up to the wheel.

"What's that on your head?" I asked.

"A captain's hat. I always wanted to wear one of these; it gives me an air of importance, don't you think?" he laughed.

"You've done it again."

"Done what?"

"Put yourself in charge; why is it you get the captain's hat?" I said with a grin.

"I'll tell you what, Pastor, it's great that we can have a good laugh together under such circumstances. Here, you have the hat."

"About time; it will look better on me anyway."

"In your dreams, Pastor."

"In all seriousness, Johnny, I wonder why He supplied a captain's hat with the clothes?"

"I wouldn't know, Pastor, but recalling how he has worked in the past, there's a reason for it and I dare say it will soon be revealed."

As the boat chugged along, I could see two guards walking along the path coming towards us. Johnny quickly dived inside the cabin. I pulled the peak of the cap down, covering as much of my face as I could. As we passed alongside them, I kept my eyes ahead so as not to make eye contact with them.

"Aye, aye, Captain!" one of the guards called out.

"Not turning, I gave them a wave. It wasn't until we were some way past that I turned. They were walking on, seemingly enjoying their stroll by the water.

"All clear. You can come out now!" I called down to Johnny.

Johnny came back alongside me. "We'll be out of the park in a couple of minutes and approaching the outskirts of London."

"Great. Hey, I think that hat did the trick. Those two guards saw what they expected, a Captain behind the wheel of a boat making its way down the canal."

"I told you the hat had a use. Now, tell me I was right."

"As usual, Johnny," I said drily.

Officer Shorts' car drew up outside the Visitors' Centre, which had been taken over as a Central Command.

"Afternoon, Sir," said the officer in control of the search.

Shorts, being dwarfed by two huge guards, strutted to the desk. Addressing the other officer, he said caustically, "Why haven't we got them?"

"Sir, there are 40 square miles of ground here - with woods, buildings and waterways; it's a lot of ground to cover with the few men I have."

"I don't want to hear excuses, man! I'm here to see them caught! I take it all road exits have been covered?"

"Yes, Sir. No one has got out; we've got them surrounded. We'll have them before nightfall, Sir."

"You say road exits; have you got the canal covered?"

There was a pause, "Er, no Sir, not the canal; I didn't think of them using that."

"How did you get to the position of officer? Find out from your men if they have seen anybody on the water, and I mean anybody!" he shouted.

199

"Yes, Sir, right away." He turned to his second-in-command.

"Who's patrolling the pathways by the canal?"

"3557 and 3887, Sir," he replied.

"Get them on the radio and ask them if they have seen anyone on the canal?"

"3557, 3887: have you observed anyone on the canal?"

"3557 here, Sir. Two boats, Sir: a man and woman on one, and a captain on the other, Sir."

Snatching the microphone, the raging Officer Shorts screamed: "What do mean, *captain?*"

"We assumed by his cap that he was, Sir."

"Did you check him out?"

"Well no, Sir. We were told to look out for two men and he was on his own. Also he was a captain, Sir."

"I don't care if he was an admiral. You were told to check everyone, and that means *everyone*. What part of 'everyone' don't you understand?"

Throwing the microphone down, he shouted to the officer in charge:

"I want those two on report and sent back to the training centre. It's highly likely the culprits have got away and have probably made it to London and *this is your fault*, man!"

With that, he stormed out of the Centre.

"London - fast!" he shouted at the driver.

200

16

"This is as far as we go, Pastor."

"Whereabouts are we?"

"We're just outside West London; if we go any further we'll be picked up by the cameras. We stand a better chance on foot. I'll pull over to the bank then you can tie the boat to a tree or stake."

As quiet as it was, Johnny checked to make sure no one was around.

"Is the boat tied?"

"She's not going anywhere. I'm ready when you are; lead the way, Johnny, I can't wait to get home," I said with excitement, even knowing the dangers that were waiting for us.

"Aren't you forgetting something, Pastor?"

"What's that?"

"The cap. If you don't want to draw attention to us, that's the worst thing you could wear, away from the water."

"I suppose you're right," I said, taking it off and throwing it on the boat.

"I'm always right, Pastor," he laughed.

Having walked across a field, we found a footpath that took us to a road. In the distance I could see a town. "What's that place?" I asked.

"Brentwood."

"Isn't that near our safe house?"

"Yes, it's the other side of town, and that's the problem. The minute we enter we'll have all the cameras to contend with. Before it didn't matter, but now they know our faces, it's not going to be easy."

"It's not my face that's the problem."

"What are you insinuating, Pastor?"

"Don't you remember, they only see what they're intended to see with my face? I think the reason we had so much trouble is yours."

"Look you, the good Lord gave me this face and He doesn't make trouble."

"There's no answer to that. Anyway, going back to you saying it's not going to be easy entering the town: With Him it will be, Johnny. We have to put our trust in Him - that He will deliver us."

I followed behind Johnny, keeping to the hedgerow and trees at the side of the road. Johnny hadn't said anything for some time, which led me to think he had something on his mind.

"Penny for your thoughts, Johnny?"

"Sorry, I was miles away. Do you ever worry, Pastor, that your time might be up?"

"I think we've had this conversation before on our adventure."

"Probably."

"No. As I said before, I'd love to be taken home to Him but if I've got to stay, then so be it. I win either way. Why do you ask?"

"Ever had a feeling that something's not right."

"Like what, Johnny?"

"That's the thing, Pastor; I don't know, but it's a strong feeling that won't go away."

"Then that's the Holy Spirit telling you something."

"Well, I wish He'd make it clear. I don't like feeling like this."

"Sometimes He does, but whatever the reason is for *not* revealing it to you, must be for your benefit. Maybe the time isn't right for it to be revealed."

"Could be."

Still keeping off the road, we followed it towards the town. The evening darkness came just in time as we entered the outskirts.

"Keep your eyes open for cameras and listening points; they're not always in the most obvious places. If you see them, keep your head down and your mouth shut, Pastor. Don't forget, the fact that it's dark doesn't make any difference; they automatically switch over to infrared.

When we get back I must ask Mordecai how he makes the face on the monitors look like the person, even though it's not them. At the moment it's beyond me but, if I can do it, I won't need Mordecai."

"That's a *big* mistake, Johnny. It's when we come before Him and say: 'I hand this over to you - it's beyond me' that He does it. It's not in *our* strength but *His*. You should try and remember that, especially in these times. We need Him more than ever."

"I know you're right, Pastor. I sometimes get carried away with things. I've got this built-in drive to problem-solve, but I have an idea, and (with a little help from above) I reckon I can do it."

"You seem confident."

"Is my name not: Johnny Gold?"

"Well no, not really."

"Point taken, Pastor."

"I was being facetious, Johnny."

We treated each street we walked along as if we were in a minefield, watching for cameras. But once again, I had confidence in Johnny. Because of his military training, I trusted that he would get us through.

Eventually he took me to the rear entrance of a house that he seemed to know.

"Who lives here?" I asked.

"A contact of mine, Pete, who has helped me out with certain things that I've needed in the past. I'm hoping he can supply us with transport."

"When was the last time you spoke to him?"

"When we went to the pens to get Linda out. He arranged for my taxi to be left in the woods for me."

"So you trust him then?"

"He's a bit of a wheeler-dealer and doesn't mind where the credits come from, but I'm pretty sure we can."

Johnny tapped on the back door. A middle-aged man came to the door and looked through the glass. Recognising Johnny, he opened the door and hushed us in. After making sure that no one had followed us, he closed the door.

Johnny made a sign that the guy obviously understood and exposed his wrist, which Johnny then scanned with his device; a green light flashed.

"We're safe to speak now," Johnny announced.

"It's been a while, my old friend. I see you made the big time on the monitors," Pete said.

"What do mean 'big time'?"

"There's a reward of 5,000 credits for information on your whereabouts. And this must be the mystery man of no name? Your friend here must be important to them; there's a 10,000 credit bounty for him."

In his usual way of making light of a serious situation, Johnny said to me, "Well you finally outdid me!" which caused us both to laugh.

"I take it there's some sort of joke between you two?" Pete asked.

"Sorry, Pete, yeah - you could say that."

"So what've you been up to? Pete enquired. "All they say is that you are wanted for crimes against humanity."

"Humanity! How can the New Order say that? They stopped showing any humanity long ago. No, we've been on a couple of assignments, abroad and here."

"I'm not even going to ask, then, if it was you that caused all the broadcasting on the screens."

"Pete, the less you know the better. This is my good friend, the Pa . . ." Johnny stopped short. "Best you don't know his name; as I said, the less you know the better all round."

"So I take it you're here because you want something?"

"I need a car, Pete; nothing that would draw attention to us."

"No problem, Johnny. You know I'm here to help if I can. Will you be going far?"

"No, it's just to get us through the town centre and on a couple of miles more to the safe house."

"And where's that?" Pete asked.

"Can I ask you why you want to know?" I asked him, not being quite as sure about him as Johnny was.

"It's always nice to know where you can take refuge if necessary."

"As Johnny said, I think it's best if you don't know the location," I replied.

"That's fine. Now, Johnny, we'd better go and get this car."

We followed him to a lock-up a few buildings away.

"Will this do?" he asked.

"That's exactly what we need," Johnny, said walking over to it. "I take it it's up-to-date on the system?"

"Of course. You won't be stopped, providing you don't do anything stupid."

"We're only travelling a few miles, so there shouldn't be any chance of that. I'll let you know where you can pick it up. How many credits do I owe you, Pete?" Johnny asked.

"Don't worry about that now; I know you're good for it. If you don't pay me, I can always turn you in and get my credits."

I gave him a serious look, which he noticed.

"Just joking, friend!" he said to me.

As Johnny drove out of the lock-up I said, "Are you sure you can trust him?"

"He's alright, Pastor. All he's interested in are credits."

"That's what bothers me; especially when he talked about turning you in. I don't think it's something to joke about."

"He wouldn't do that. We go back a long way, and even if he did, by the time he informs on us we'll be in the safe house. But I don't think he will."

"Johnny, I don't have to remind you what the Bible says about the last days, when even brother will turn against brother?"

"I know what it says, Pastor, but I just cannot see Pete doing that to me."

"I pray you're right Johnny."

"Hello. I've got information on the a whereabouts of the two people you are looking for."

"Please hold; you are being connected to the right department," piped the voice at the other end of the phone.

"You say you have information on the two wanted men?" came a man's voice.

"Yes, they have just broken into my home and forced me to give them my car keys," he said, sounding upset.

"Slow down while we confirm a few details. Answer yes or no. According to your signal, your name is: Peter Atterbury, ID number: 890366651?"

"Yes."

"Your registered place of residence is: 555 Long Avenue, Brentwood, State Area 4?"

"Yes."

"The system shows that there was a malfunction with your transmitter; can you tell us why?"

"No, Sir."

"We'll look into it. Mr Atterbury, you say the two men in question broke into your home and demanded your vehicle."

"Yes, I tried to resist but they were aggressive and threatened my life."

"Just answer 'yes' or 'no', Mr Atterbury."

"Yes."

"So when did this happen?"

"Just now."

"How do you know they are the two we're after?"

"I've seen them on the monitor screens that the system's been broadcasting. It's definitely them."

"Do you know what direction they took?"

"Yes, I overheard one of them say that they didn't have far to go and were heading to the other side of town."

"We have two vehicles registered to you: PA15 and PA16. Which one did they take?"

"PA16."

"Please confirm that there has been no attempt to disengage it from the system by yourself or anyone?"

"No. I wouldn't do that, knowing there's an automatic confinement for it."

"Just yes or no, Mr Atterbury."

"No."

"The New Order thanks you, Mr Atterbury; your co-operation has been recorded."

"What about the credits, the reward?"

The line went dead.

"Sir, a report's just come in of a sighting of the two."

Getting up from his desk, Officer Shorts said impatiently, "At last! Whereabouts, man?"

Because he knew that the officer in charge of London HQ had intercepted the train, in the hope of capturing them before he did, he bribed one of his men in Communications to let him know if anything came in on the two.

"Brentwood, Sir, and their car is being tracked."

"At last - today I've got them! Have my car brought round, and hurry," he said with a grin of anticipation on his face.

"Yes, Sir, right away."

17

"**H**ome at last! You go on in. I'll get rid of the car. Tell them to get the coffee on."

"Are you going to be okay on your own? After all, I wouldn't want you to get into trouble - as I'm not with you to get you out of it."

"Yeah, sure. Actually, Pastor, putting all joking to one side, we made a pretty good team, didn't we?"

"We sure did, Johnny. You know, I think we could be good friends (despite your chuckles)."

"That's part of what friends do, Pastor - laugh together. Can I tell you something?"

"What's that?"

"I haven't laughed so much in my life as I have since I met you."

"All I can say, Johnny, is we can thank the Lord for that."

"Now, Pastor, I know you can't bear to be apart from me, but haven't you got a wife in there that you haven't seen for some time?"

"I certainly have. I'll see you soon."

"Linda, they're back!" Mark shouted as he released the door.

As I went in Linda came running, threw her arms round me and kissed me.

"I missed you so much! I'm not letting you out of my sight again," she said, leading me to our room without giving me a chance to greet everyone.

"Pastor!" Mark called after me, "Where's Johnny?"

"Getting rid of the car; he shouldn't be long."

Johnny found a place to dump the car a few streets away and was walking back, when the feeling that something was wrong came upon him. But what, he didn't know. All he knew was that he had a sense of urgency to get back.

Everyone was busy, getting the food ready and setting the long table for a celebratory meal. The children were making a banner to say 'Welcome Home', when, without any warning, the blast from an explosion ripped the steel door open. Mark and several of the others who had their backs to the door were blown across the room. The deafening noise brought Linda and me running to see what had happened.

To my horror, there in the smoke that filled the room were two huge State guards with guns. As the smoke settled, in strutted a small officer. I instantly recognised him; it was the one Johnny called 'The Squirt'. The children were screaming hysterically and he gave them a venomous look.

He said to his two men, "Shut that noise up."

The two men opened fire on the children. I stood there in disbelief, shocked to the core at what had just happened.

"Ah, *at last* - we finally catch up with each other and you have a chance to answer some long overdue questions before I eliminate you. You are a person of mystery to me; I cannot find you on the system. Apparently you don't exist. How come?"

"I'll not tell you anything, you monster!"

"Shoot the two women over there," he said calmly to his men.

Before I had a chance to say anything, the room was filled with the sound of gunfire. The two women lay dead.

"Shall we try that again? Now, who are you?"

"I knew that, even if I told him, the heartless man was going to kill us all. I looked at Mark who was lying on the floor, wounded from the blast.

"Don't tell him, Pastor," he gasped.

Shorts walked over to him and, at point blank range, shot him.

"If there's one thing I dislike, it's being interrupted while I'm speaking; but then you lowlifes don't know any better," he said. "So you are a pastor? A prize catch! This will go well for me when I report back - that I've disposed of a pastor. So, Pastor, what do they call you? Pastor what?"

I couldn't have told him even if I wanted to. I was in complete shock over what had just taken place.

"Not going to tell me? Kill them all."

I just had time to look at the others, and each of them looked calm and unafraid. Like me, they didn't fear death - as we all knew that, in an instant, we would be transported to the presence of the Lord.

Yet I wasn't going to go without my final say.

213

"Do your worst, little man. These people here are far bigger than you could ever be, even if you think that having big guys beside you makes you big."

I could see that made him angry.

Linda gripped me as she stood behind me. I closed my eyes expecting death. The guns went off but I felt nothing.

I slowly opened my eyes to see that they had shot everyone, except Linda and me.

"Why didn't you shoot us?"

"Oh no, that would spoil the fun for me; you see I'm a man who gets his way. This pretty lowlife hiding behind you, Pastor, wouldn't be your wife would she? I promised my two men here a little reward if we caught you and the other lowlife."

"Well you may have me but you don't have my friend," I said trying to distract his attention from Linda.

"Oh, that's where you're wrong! You see, we know he is on his way here. The tracker in the car you used led us right to you. I *said* you would make a mistake, in your desperation to get to your so-called home. You were very careless in not realising that the car had a tracker and, of course, there was my inspired idea of posting a large reward for the pair of you. That, my friend, is what brought your downfall."

I felt hopeless. I had no way of warning Johnny about what he was walking into. *Lord,* I prayed, *give him discernment that something's wrong.*

"Now, back to that pretty little wife of yours. She's all yours men," he said.

I dragged Linda into our room and slammed the door, thinking for one crazy moment that would stop them harming her.

The door burst open. "You see, Pastor Lowlife, there's nowhere to go. Now maybe, just maybe, I might surprise myself and let her live. Now, your *name*? And that's the last time I'm going to ask!"

I positioned myself between them and Linda, then I took her in my arms and held her tightly.

"Forgive them, Father. We're ready to come into your presence. I love you, Linda."

"I love you too"

"I take it that's a 'no'? Shoot them!"

The sound of my name being called made me open my eyes. Standing in front of me, in an aura of light, was a figure with long, golden hair and dressed in a shimmering translucent robe. It was Aquila.

"Come, Christian; He is waiting for you," she said giving me her hand.

I looked around for Linda but couldn't see her.

"Where's Linda?" I asked.

"She is already there."

"Where's 'there'?"

"Home, Christian; your Heavenly home. Now we have to go; He is waiting."

"You look different without your armour," I said, taking her hand.

"I only wear it when I battle evil forces. This is my usual raiment and it is how you will see me in the future."

I had a sensation of travelling at great speed. I had no concept time. One second I was standing there reaching out for her hand, and then I was in front of a dazzling light that seemed to be alive.

From within the light, a soft voice called my name, "Christian, come."

I could feel myself gliding into the light, and in it I could see the form of a man. As I looked into His eyes, love poured from them and bathed my whole being – so much that I felt as though I could melt at His feet in overwhelming adoration.

He spoke, "Well done, my faithful friend; your reward will be great."

I felt myself moving through the light, to be brought before a group of people. I instantly recognised them. They were my loved ones and friends. All I could hear were the words, "Welcome home! Welcome home! As I passed through the group, in front of me was a glowing mist where I could just make out that someone was moving towards me.

"Christian, it's me - Linda."

Yes, it was my Linda; as beautiful as the day I first met her, young with long flowing hair.

"You promised me that walk, Christian, she said taking my hand.

Johnny stood outside the safe house. Alarm bells rang inside, as he could see that the steel door had been blown open.

Cautiously he stepped in; his fears confirmed by the scene that lay before him. Around the room were the bodies of his friends, lying where they had fallen. As he couldn't see the Pastor or Linda he walked over to their room, to find the door partly open. He gave it a gentle push, to reveal the two of them dead on the floor. By their position he could see that Christian had tried to protect Linda.

Looking down at them, he said, "Farewell, my good friend. In the brief time I knew you, you brought out the laughter in me. Mordecai sure was right about that. It was an honour knowing you, Pastor."

It was obvious that they had all been taken by surprise, as no one had attempted to use the escape exit. Numb with shock, he was checking to see if there was the slim chance of anyone still being alive, when he heard a voice behind him.

"Your sentiments over these lowlifes will have me in tears. *Big* mistake - coming here, lowlife! You have led me quite a chase, in two countries, and you have been an inconvenience to me from the start. But it's all over for you now; and you will end up like your friends here."

It was The Squirt, accompanied by two men with their automatic guns aimed at Johnny, and waiting for the order to fire.

"Stand down, men. I'm going to award *myself* the pleasure of shooting him." He took out his pistol and pointed it at Johnny.

"I thought you had orders from the Supreme One to bring me in alive?" Johnny said, trying to buy some time while he edged himself to the back of the room.

"What? Try taking you back to Israel and give you the chance of escaping again? What do you take me for, stupid?"

"Well, you said it."

Johnny had backed up towards the secret escape door.

Suddenly the room filled with a blinding light and Mordecai appeared.

"Go, Johnny. I've got it under control."

Johnny wasted no time in activating the escape door and made his way down to the high-speed boat.   He felt the building starting to shake. Quickly he made the outer steel roller-door open and sped down the river. A roaring sound made him turn, to see the building collapsing into a pile of rubble.

Johnny disappeared into the distance, knowing that, because he didn't die with his friends, he was saved for a purpose. That could only mean there was another assignment waiting ahead for him . . .